The Queen's Runner

A Swashbuckling Lesbian Erotica

Episode 2:
The Magic Touch

by

D.B. Francais

The Magic Touch © 2014 by D.B. Francais
Episode 2 of *The Queen's Runner*
Proserpian Press
ISBN: 9780998986609

Cover art:
iStock.com/sundrawalex (front cover)
(Back cover image photographed by the author)

Foreword From the Author

This story was written purely as escapist fun and by no means attempts to sneak a hidden message or cause into the reader's mind. While it is almost guaranteed that someone can find a moral somewhere to extract from this story, doing so is not advised.

However, should the reader decide to go ahead and find one anyway, it is the sincere wish of the author that they at least pick one of the good ones and handle it lightly.

To King Pontus of Proserpia, urgent

Dear Father,

Let me begin with an apology. I know I must have worried you and my siblings terribly by now, and for that I am deeply sorry. Current events have been passing strange for me lately, but suffice it to say that circumstances unforeseen have brought me for the first time to the surface, where I am experiencing many new, often wondrous events and learning quite a good deal about myself in the process.

I know what that must sound like, but please, I implore you, fret not for me or my safety. I am here now of my own will and accord, safe and unmolested, and do plan to continue as such for a while yet. Know, however, that I am free to return home whensoever I choose, and shall do so once I have seen my fill of life above water. I regret if this should cause you yet further worry, but you have my most heartfelt assurance that I am in good hands and good company. So long as it is conceivably possible, I shall not come to harm before I return to you all. What my punishment may be once I do so I leave to your wisdom.

With all my love and respect,

Lorelei,
Sixth princess of Proserpia

***

"Safe *and* unmolested?" my Captain's voice mocks over my shoulder. "Lorelei, you little liar, you..."

"Relatively," I argue with a stark blush. "And the technicalities of the matter do not merit discussion with one's father or siblings."

She chuckles at that, that low, throaty sound of amusement she has that makes me quiver a little inside, then wraps her arms around me from behind and slides her head over my shoulder. With a finger and a casual air of entitlement, she turns my face to hers, finding my lips with her own and letting them linger a while. Her ample chest I feel pressed warm and bare against my shoulder blades, and her free hand slips my strapless sundress down past my own small breasts before cupping one and simply holding it, firm and gentle and possessive. None of this helps with my blush, but I imagine that she realizes this even if it is not, against all prior evidence, one of the motivations for her actions.

Her hands and lips and presence release me just as my letter slips from my hands. She smiles and reaches forward, snatching it from the air before it can drift down to the deck, then spins on her heel and strides away across the ship with it. Self-consciously I adjust my dress, tugging it back up over my now-sensitized breasts, though this is more of an affectation of normalcy than for any practical purpose of modesty; after almost two weeks of being held captive on *The Queen's Runner,* there is no longer any part of me that my captor Captain Vine has not seen or felt.

These past few days especially, she has even had my permission. Not that she has ever needed or asked for it thus far. Still, she always seemed to end up with it by the end, even from the beginning, though I never actually granted it. Or not exactly. Not in the strictest sense of the word.

It is … complicated.

"'*Sixth* princess?'" she asks, turning back to me and waving my letter, eyebrows raised. She still has not put her clothes back on since removing them a few nights ago to bandage her wounds, so she stands before me now wearing only her ever-present talisman of pale wood hanging on a necklace between her breasts. If she even knows what modesty means, she decided against it long before I ever met her. It does make conversation hard at times, but I am learning. "You have five other brothers and sisters?"

"No," I say, taking my letter back, "I am the sixth *princess*. I have five other *sisters*." Carefully, I roll the parchment into a tight cylinder and slip it into the empty bottle she's found for me among the scant supplies left on our ship after Rockquay. "I only have three brothers."

"Sweet Mother," she mutters. "You sure this is even necessary, then? How are they gonna even notice you're gone with that many of them?"

"Because I am the youngest," I explain, sitting down beneath the mast. "I am the most pampered, the most sheltered, the least expected to do anything reckless or foolhardy. If any of my brothers or a number of my sisters were to go missing for a few days, we would assume that they have gone to explore the realm and fret not. If *I* am absent for even a full night, the rest of them assume — not without good reason — that I have gotten myself lost and require aid."

"Hmm," is the entirety of my Captain's reply. She watches me thoughtfully for a moment, then strides purposefully toward me. I brace myself for another sudden onslaught of her spontaneous affection, but instead she leaps nimbly up over my head and scurries up the mast like a crab into its hiding hole. Left alone and un-fondled on the deck for the moment, I return to the task at hand.

There are four final components left to this package I am assembling: the two alabaster scallop shells I wore upon first surfacing, a water-proof bottle stopper to which to fasten them, a length of thin but sturdy string with which to fasten them, and my discarded fin. Captain Vine assures me that I no longer need it for any practical purpose, that I will grow a new one when I allow my legs to form back into a tail. I have decided to trust her in this; so far, at least, everything else she has told me about the world outside my scope of experience has been proven true, even a few things about myself that I did not know before our meeting.

And in any event, a fin is of little compensation on a tail without scales, and my old scales are long since lost beyond our acquisition, unfairly confiscated by the port authority back at Rockquay along with my Captain's wardrobe, our supplies of food, and everything else of obvious value onboard that could be lifted and removed. I shall either grow everything back or none of it, logic suggests, so this one dried-up part of me does me no good either way.

I roll my fin into a loose cylinder and slip it into the bottle as well around the note, then set to tying both shells to the stopper. Hopefully, when all is done and my message is dropped into the last place where my sisters saw me, it will be recognized as a clue to my whereabouts as opposed to regular surface flotsam. It is not a brilliant plan, I realize, but I must let my family know what has become of me and that I am safe — and my only other option is to return home and inform them personally, but if I do that I am afraid I will not come back. Either Father will forbid it, and understandably so, or else I shall simply … lose my nerve. I confess I have never really had it until just recently, and I am not yet sure how confident I am in its hold. I am not yet sure of many things, not least of which that I am even here now for any good or sound reason. Captain Vine has freely admitted that part of the draw I feel toward her is sorcerous in nature, a charming enchantment innate to her people that she cannot entirely enforce or revoke. And she has offered to return me to my home of her own free will and end my bondage to her if I but choose it. And, on that note, I *am* technically a victim of abduction and hostage…

"Hey, Lei!" Captain calls from the rigging high above my head. "Pretty sure we're here!"

But it is an old argument, one I have had with myself daily since this ordeal began. I am sure I will continue to have it with myself in the days to come. So far, I have managed to produce only a scant few answers to the many questions it generates. They are enough for now.

"Almost done!" I call back, tying off the last knot and sealing the bottle as my Captain descends from the ropes with all the natural grace of a bird in flight coming in to roost.

When I have answers to all of my questions, then I will carry them home with me. This is my decision, and for now I will adhere to it.

***

After night falls, and after my care package is in the water and we are well away, my Captain comes to my bedroom in the cabin as usual. Tonight, however, I am not chained to the headboard as a precaution against my escaping in the middle of the night. It is no longer necessary; I have just proven my resolve to remain of my own will, at least for a time. So the silver tether remains coiled on the floor by the mattress, one end still attached to the simple wooden frame — the Rockquay port authority was not able to remove it to have it spirited away with the rest of the ship's goods, and apparently even they were not so cruel as to have the bed hauled away.

Tonight, instead, my Captain brings with her the length of red cloth which she wore ashore wrapped around her breasts as a top, now one of her only articles of clothing along with her knee-length pants and knee-high leather boots.

I think nothing of it at first, and think even less as my Captain intercepts whatever comment I am about to make by grabbing the back of my head and crushing her lips to mine. She pulls away just long enough to grab the hem of my sundress and yank it up and off, over my head, then wraps it around the back of my shoulders and pulls me forward to continue where she left off.

I am used to this by now. Her affections are not always this sudden and urgent, but they manifest that way often enough that, though they usually catch me off guard, I am rarely surprised by them anymore.

What does surprise me is when I feel her hands grip my wrists and cross them behind my back, then deftly wrap my dress around them. I pull my lips away in confusion, turning to look over my shoulder as she finishes tying off her knot. "What?" I breathe, trying to tug my arms apart. This makeshift bind is soft, but it holds firm. "Captain, why are —"

"Shh." She puts a slender finger to my lips, silencing me. "I'm not done yet." With the same smirk that always precedes our intimacy, she takes up her chest wrap, folds it once over itself, and presses the fabric to my eyes. I pull away on instinct, but her hands are quicker than my reflexes, reaching behind my head to tie another knot there, blindfolding me.

"Is this necessary?" I protest. "I thought we had settled the matter of my staying. Do you not trust my resolve in this?"

"Lorelei, I trust you more than I've let myself trust anyone in a long, long time," she answers from the now-darkness in front of me. "So no, strictly speaking, this is not necessary. But it is fun."

I frown. "I do not see how this is supposed to be enjoyable from my perspective."

"No? Have you forgotten already?" I feel her finger caressing my collarbone, soft and light, like the brush of swimming through a grove of kelp. "Our first kiss? Your first time? You were wrapped up pretty similarly, as I recall." Her fingers slip up my neck to my chin, making me tilt my head back on instinct, and I can feel the warmth of her breath, the closeness of her face, as I lift mine on her subtle, tactile command.

Has she … is she *training* me to respond to her like this? I barely even notice all the little ways I submit to her throughout our average day together. How deep is her hold on me, and how long have I been reinforcing it?

"You toy with me," I accuse, my voice weak and quavering already. "You always play with me as if I were some sort of doll here to amuse you."

"Yes," she whispers warm against my lips. "And not once have you told me that you didn't like it or asked me to stop."

I swallow as my face starts to burn. No longer her heat — this is all mine now, starting at my cheeks and leaking slowly down through the rest of my body. But she is masterful at summoning it.

She chuckles and brushes a hand across my sizzling cheek. "That's why I picked you up in the first place, remember? To be my toy and cheer me up." I take a deep, shuddery breath, leaning my face into her palm. She chuckles again and continues. "And while I am extremely glad that we've become friends somehow since then, you're still my doll, Lorelei. You chose to stay with me, and you knew that meant you would still be mine. All mine," she breathes, "from here …"

Her fingers brush my lips, which part with a ragged gasp, then move on.

"… to here …"

Her hand slips down my neck and over my chest, cupping one soft, small breast on its way and kneading it once, slowly.

"… to, mmm, especially to here …"

My legs part gently of their own volition at her impending arrival, not waiting for my permission, knowing with a certainty built on experience that it will come later, much later, when my mind is under my own power once more. Her fingers part and slip down around the edges of my new lips, the heat from her skin warm as her hand sinks to cover the swelling petals.

It is quickly becoming unbearable. I do not need any more heat anywhere on my body, least of all there; I already burn with a throbbing wet insistency, and the proximity of her touch — close, so close, but not *quite* close enough, not actually touching — only exasperates my torment until my legs start to squirm beneath me. I lean my hips forward to meet her hand, but she just as gradually pulls it away, keeping her skin a breath away from my own, her fingertips only lightly planted on the very edge of my molten need. I whimper (I *whimper!* I, a royal princess and a mature young woman! How has it come to this?) and make to reach for her hand, to force the contact. I end up tugging at my binds in confusion for several seconds before I remember and realize why my arms are suddenly powerless, and the resultant moan of disappointment sounds pitiful even to my own ears.

Captain Vine laughs low in her throat from a few inches in front of me. "I see you remember after all," she purrs, her other hand tracing a slow line up the small of my back and back down again. "Does it displease you, Princess? Shall I stop?"

"N-no …!" I gasp, then blush anew with shame to hear the base urgency in my voice. Still, that does not stop me. "Captain …" I breathe, chest starting to heave, words beginning to desert me. "P-please …"

"Please what, my little pearl?" she asks, drawing a quick circle around the focus of my agony with the tip of a finger, making me lift and buck my entire lower half in a desperate attempt to catch it. No such luck. "Please play with you like a doll?"

I bite my lower lip, focusing on breathing.

"Please remind you that you belong to me?"

I swallow again and, as much as I dare, bob my head in a quick, hasty nod.

"Lorelei." Her voice is a soft command, a pillow with a core of stone, and behind it I hear that intolerable smirk of hers. "Say it."

I open my mouth. My breath escapes in a quick succession of ragged pants. I lick my lips, swallow again, and rein in my lungs just long enough to whisper, "P … please make m-me … your t-toy, Captain … please …"

For a long moment, nothing happens except that I feel what's left of my pride burn within my chest at each successive indignation that I force it through. Then I feel Captain Vine's lips at my ear. "Good girl," she whispers, and then my sightless world tilts as she pushes me back, my back hitting the mattress at the same moment that one of her fingers slips deep inside of me and curls tightly.

The sound I make is somewhere between a moan and a wordless cry for help and, I think, probably the loudest noise my lungs have yet produced since I began using them. I can feel my burning need clench tight around her finger inside of me, my hips struggling upward toward the contact, my legs trembling in indecision whether to close shut on her hand to prevent it from leaving or open wider to give her better access. My hands, pinned beneath my back, grip the bed sheets tightly as if they are the only thing keeping me from falling upward into this burning sea of desire.

Then her finger begins to prod harder, rubbing quick circles around the small wall of flesh she has curled it against, each pass sending a wave of undiluted pleasure crashing over me. I cry out again, just as loud as before, grip tightening until I can feel the blood draining from my knuckles.

It is too much. Frantically I try to push myself away from her on the bed with only my trembling legs, already half-paralyzed by the sensations crashing through me, threatening to suffocate me in a red-hot whirlpool of unbearable ecstasy. I scramble a few inches back, but she follows, her attention unrelenting. I shake my head rapidly, trying to convey some sense of the urgency I do not have power to speak. As much as I needed her touch a few moments ago, now I desperately need her to stop before it swallows me whole.

She laughs that deep, throaty laugh of hers and rubs even faster.

"Aaaahh!" My legs collapse, quivering, useless. My lower body jerks and writhes wildly, without direction, sometimes into her touch, sometimes away from it. She keeps up, her finger never leaving that one spot inside of me. My breath skips, stops for a moment, redoubles. My lungs cannot take the strain. My body cannot take the heat. I am going to melt. I am going to burst.

My Captain says something to me. I do not know what. I think it is a question, so I thrash my head back and forth in answer. Whatever she is asking, all I know is that I cannot take one more moment beneath her touch, one more —

Her tongue flicks across the little bud just above her probing finger.

I shove myself hard as I can against her mouth, her finger, and cry out without breath or sound as I break beneath the agonizing pleasure and melt away into a molten puddle on the bed.

What feels like hours pass as I float there, wet and dripping, senseless but for the paralyzing current of ecstasy searing its way through me, consuming me, washing me away. Finally the intensity begins to slowly lessen, and little bits of me begin to wash up from the burning sea I had just drowned in. I become aware of my own breathing once more, shaky and quick and as deep as I can manage for now, gulping down desperate lungfuls of air until my throat feels raw with overuse. I become aware of my limbs, trembling and useless, my arms a tingling lump pressing into my back, my legs splayed and half numb and feeling as if they belong to somebody else. I become aware of my sight, which is still locked away behind my blindfold so that all I can see is a dull red glow through the fabric.

And I become aware of my Captain, whose tongue has been slowly lapping up the full length of my lower lips for I don't know how long, the tip flicking over the small bud at the top with each pass and sending lingering jolts of pleasure through my already racked and spent body.

"Ca … Captain …" I manage to gasp out. "What are y …?"

"Mmhmhmhm," she chuckles against my quivering sex, and the resulting hum against my tender flesh sends a slow writhe all the way through me. "You're soaked," she says quietly, hot breath on my skin. "I'm cleaning up the mess you made."

"But …" But she has already gone back to licking me, and with each stroke of her tongue I feel the heat building anew. "W-wait…!" I moan. Again? Already? My gods, is this woman trying to kill me with pleasure? There is absolutely no way my body can stand another round of her fun so soon after the last!

"Hm?" Her tongue stops on my little bud, circles it once, then she asks, "Something you want to say, my little toy?"

"No … no more …" I pant feebly, gulping to try and ease the feeling of rawness in my throat. "I can't …"

"You can't play with me anymore?" she asks, then slowly slides her tongue the full length of my throbbing lips once more, making me gasp. "But I'm not ready to put my doll away just yet." And her tongue slips inside of me.

The only thing keeping me from pushing myself deeper into her mouth is that I lack the energy. Instead I bite my lip to stifle another moan and lie there beneath her, passively surrendering to her appetite, unable to stop her or my own reaction as my body betrays me once more, welcoming her in and clinging tightly to her probing tongue to try and keep her from leaving again.

It feels so incredibly good, I can't stand it. Every time she forces me into deeper pleasure than I can bear, then makes me bear it regardless and smiles at my torment. I hate it, and I love it, and I hate how much I love it, and I can't help it.

Before long it returns, the inescapable ecstasy that pins me down helpless and has its way with me. I no longer know where my body ends and her mouth begins when it crashes over me once more, the whole of me tensing and clenching as the burning wetness courses through me and into her, then shuddering back down as the biggest waves pass and I drift along on the aftermath. Captain Vine keeps her mouth pressed firmly to me throughout the whole of it, drinking me in and coaxing me onward until I am completely spent, my mind enwrapped in a warm fog that feels only distantly connected to the rest of me.

I am floating inside this warm, damp cloud when she finally pulls her mouth away from me, and I feel the mattress sink as she crawls over the full length of my body. Her soft breasts brush past my own, then press down against them as she lowers herself to me, her hair draping to brush against my cheek. I can taste her breath on my own as I pant beneath her, and when she speaks, I can hear the smile in her voice. "Helplessness looks good on you," she says quietly, her fingers brushing her hair and my own from my face. "You're so beautiful, my little pearl."

I blush anew, but before I can reply, her lips are pressed to mine and her tongue is inside my mouth now, teasing my own and coaxing it out between both of our lips. I can taste myself in her kiss, warm and slick and intimate. It is passing strange to taste oneself, especially on another, but it is not unpleasant. And on my parched lips, my mouth ragged from everything it has been through because of her, her kiss is pleasantly refreshing.

She pulls away then, leaving my lips parted and my tongue out as I catch my breath she has stolen. The warm weight of her chest lifts from mine, and I feel her thighs on my sides move closer, until her own soft wetness brushes past my hardened nipples and stops just before my open mouth. "Now it's your turn to play with me," she says from above, threading her fingers into my hair. "You don't need me to take that blindfold off or untie you just yet, do you?"

I lick my lips and swallow the last taste of myself that she left behind. "No, Captain."

"Good," she says with a chuckle, pressing herself to my lips. "Then show me who you belong to, little doll."

"Yes, Captain," I answer. And I do.

***

Afterwards, after my Captain unties me and takes off my blindfold, she curls up in the bed beside me and falls asleep. For a moment, I wonder what to do — for despite our intimacy and the time we've spent together so far, we have never shared a night together. Every night, after whatever exertions our day held, I was retired to the bedroom with my chain and there fell asleep alone, my Captain leaving me to spend the night … elsewhere, I suppose, though I know not where. She has told me that this is the only such room on her ship; her only other options would be the small galley, the small closet, or the open deck, none of which seem like particularly comfortable places to spend a whole night asleep.

Or there is below deck, I suppose, though I know not what is down there. Captain Vine hasn't been secretive about it so much as simply not volunteering the information, and it has never occurred to me before to ask. Perhaps she retires to some cozy nook down there.

It occurs to me now that I may have displaced her from her usual sleeping quarters when I took over this room, but the thought does not move much guilt in me. The idea, after all, was her own. And also I did not ask nor consent to being a passenger on this ship when the arrangement was made, of course. Strange that I must remember that now, rather than it being on the forefront of my mind.

I soon grow to relax and set my worries aside — no small feat not so long ago, but it is becoming surprisingly easier the longer I spend up here. As I feel my own fatigue catch up to me, feel the pleasant, dull soreness of what is becoming our routine take over my limbs, I lie back in bed myself and close my eyes. Next to me, Captain Vine breathes in a deep rhythm in time with the rocking of the ship and the muted creak of waves on wood. It is calming, soothing, and I soon find myself curled up on my side, snuggled closer to her naked back, my face resting on her spilled curtain of dark brown hair on the edge of our only pillow. She smells of salt spray and warm breezes, the sea and the wind, memories both old and new. I smile as I drift off, wrapped in tender nostalgia, and drape an arm over my peaceful Captain to hold the feeling close as the first tides of sleep wash over me.

But at my touch, my Captain stiffens suddenly, her breathing cut off with a sharp intake as her whole body suddenly goes rigid and unmoving. The change is enough to draw me back awake again, and I blink, startled, careful to make no sudden movements. "Captain?" I whisper against her hair. "Is something wrong?"

There is a moment of tenseness, then Captain Vine exhales in one long, ragged sigh, her body relaxing back into the mattress. One of her hands covers mine against her abdomen, and I can feel her fingers trembling slightly against my own. "No," she mumbles, still facing away from me. "Sorry. I was half asleep already. For a moment I … I forgot it was you."

I pull my hand from beneath hers and rest it on top, holding her hand gently as the last of the trembling dies away. "Who else would it be, Captain?" I ask.

I hear a faint, sleepy version of her usual amused chuckle, then her hand turns in mine to cup it gently and hold it close. "Who else indeed?" she mutters, just on the edge of hearing. "You're right. Sorry to worry you, Lorelei."

Were I more awake right now, I might pursue this further. But my energy is spent, and my bed is soft, and my Captain is warm against my skin. "It's okay, Captain," I murmur back into the curtain of her hair.

"Sleep well, my little pearl," I hear her say through dark, muffled waters.

"Goodnight," I think I reply, but I cannot be sure, for now the currents have closed over me and I willingly let them drag me down from myself to the warm seafloor of sleep.

***

"Welp … we've got a bit of an issue, turns out," Captain Vine announces the next day as she comes up from the ship's hold and out onto the deck.

I turn from staring out over the railing to ask what she means, then gasp as she steps into the sunlight. She has removed her bandages from her thigh and wrists, and while the sword gash in her thigh is little more than a thin red line now and healing visibly clean, both of her wrists are chafed bright red and swollen, the skin beginning to peel in little ragged edges. “Captain!” I exclaim, rushing to her and taking one of her hands in mine, turning her wrist up to better note the damage. “Gods below, what has happened to you?”

“Oh, this?” She prods the enflamed flesh with a finger, wincing slightly. “Yeah, well, there’s that too, I guess. Should probably get that looked at soon.”

“You guess?” I repeat, a bit harsher than I intended. “Captain, I think these wounds have surpassed the capabilities of a mere bandage. Was this done to you in prison?”

She takes her hand back from my grip, examining her own wrists more closely and smiling a tight smile that doesn’t reach her eyes. “Iron burn,” she answers. “From the shackles they arrested me with. They were only on about half an hour as they dragged me through town to my cell, but that long in direct contact eats in pretty deep, apparently.”

I stare at the wounds in worried awe. To put it bluntly, they look a bit disgusting. “All of this from touching a metal?” I ask. “I knew it caused you discomfort, but I never imagined such a thing would cause this much damage.”

“Yeah, well, the closest equivalent I’ve found so far is like touching the heart of a fire. Don’t suppose you’ve ever done that?”

I shake my head. “We do not have fire underwater, Captain.”

“Right, figured as much. Well, if you ever get the chance, I don’t recommend it.” She gingerly pokes at her wounds a moment longer before shaking her head and dropping her hands to her sides. "Anyway, that's not what's most important right now, though I'll add it to the list. Remember how we docked in Rockquay because I said the ship needed some repairs done?"

"Yes?" I say cautiously. The list? When she began she said we only had a bit of a single issue. Now there are enough to warrant a list?

"Yes. Well, between our being arrested and breaking out again, it seems we never got around to that. So now the ship needs a few more repairs done." She sighs and crosses her arms, turning her head to gaze out at the open sea. "And while we're in a noticing impending problems mood, I should probably also point out that we're out of food."

I frown. "Completely?" I ask.

She shrugs. "We've got a couple of bruised apples and a small bushel of slimeroot that I think they mistook for a sack of putrefying refuse."

"Slimeroot?" My nose wrinkles instinctively at the word.

"It's just what it sounds like," Captain Vine answers with a grimace. "Tastes about like what you'd expect, too. But it's nutritious and takes upwards of three years to start decaying, so I grabbed some for emergency rations in case a situation like this turned up." She turns on her heel then and climbs up to the roof of the cabin, where the ship's wheel stands prominently overlooking the deck. "All the same, though, I'd prefer to make landfall again as soon as possible so we can put off having to eat any for as long as we can."

"Captain," I call up to her, "out of curiosity, what all provisions *do* we have left? The port authority seized all of our goods worth having, I had thought."

"You want the full list?" she asks, leaning on the wheel and gazing down at me. "Besides the bit of food I just mentioned, we've got a couple more empty bottles like the one you threw overboard the other day, a handful of tattered rags, the bedroom furniture, two lengths of silver chain, and the clothes we escaped in. Oh," she adds, brightening a moment, "and what we stole from confiscation on our way out. My sword and a few pocketfuls of coins. So, silver lining, there's that."

"So provided we find another town here soon," I continue, "we should have enough money to see to both the ship's and our own needs?"

"Um … no." She turns the wheel slowly, hand over hand, then stops and slouches against it, frowning. "We can restock our food provisions, maybe get a couple of new outfits to give the ones we have now a break, and not much else. Or we could get a handful of minor repairs done to the ship. But we definitely can't afford everything we need just yet."

"Then … how are we to remedy this?" I ask hesitantly.

She turns to face the waves in the direction of the rising sun, takes a deep breath, holds it for a moment, then slowly lets it out again through her nose. She says nothing.

"… Captain Vine?" I ask again after a few seconds.

"I'm still working that one out," she says quietly, barely audible above the breeze and the lap of the waves. "I'm a be honest, I've thought of dipping you back in the ocean until you grow more scales for us to harvest, but it's probably not very healthy to do that over and over, not to mention I'd feel like an exploitative bitch if we went that route again so soon. Only cuz it's you." She turns toward the sun again as if to check that it's still there, adjusts the wheel slightly, then releases it. "Maybe we can find some quick and easy work to do when we get to where we're going," she adds as she climbs down to the deck.

"Where *are* we going, anyway?" I ask. I am beginning to realize just how little I'm actually involved with the ship that I've been living on these past weeks. Captain Vine had been doing everything herself before we'd met, so I had been letting her continue as such, but now I'm wondering if I shouldn't take a more active role somehow.

"Due north," she says, crossing the deck to lean out over the prow. I follow. "They took my map too, so I'm not sure where all the major landmarks and towns around us are, but I know the general layout of the islands and landmasses. Rockquay is to the west, on the tip of a peninsula that juts southward from a continent to our north." She pulls her head back from bending over the railing to flash me a reassuring smile. "So we're gonna head north to the coast, steering well away from any area where we may conceivably be recognized as wanted fugitives, then float eastward along the land's edge once we find it until we spot the first town with a harbor. Should only take a few days at this clip."

"Do we have enough food to last us until then?"

Her smile instantly inverts. "By 'last us,' do you mean 'survive on,' or 'stay well fed with?'"

"Either."

"Oh, yeah, we're not gonna starve," she says with a shake of her head. "I'm a light eater, and from what I've seen, so are you. We're just gonna go hungry here real soon is all." She runs a hand through the waves of her hair and draws her mouth into a pensive line. "'Course, you could always jump overboard and go fishing if you get so inclined, and I'll haul you back up when you're done. Not really a fan of fish meat myself, unfortunately."

"That would mean growing and shedding another tail," I remind her. "I thought you said I ought not to do that too rapidly?"

"Right. We'll see what necessity dictates, I guess. And then, well … there's always the slimeroot …"

***

In the end, we resort to the slimeroot — a pinch each, a small wad of oozing vegetation rolled into a ball about the size of a shucked oyster. It looks like rotting kelp covered in a film of slug juice, and it smells like the inside of a gutted manatee left to bake in the sun. I balk at the smell, but by now my stomach is growling so loudly that I judge it worth the effort. Captain Vine recommends that I pinch my nose shut and swallow the wad whole to minimize the experience, but even then I gag getting it down, and it takes drinking near a gallon of water just to get the taste from my mouth. My Captain does not have even this comfort as, she informs me, few land-living creatures can stomach seawater in even moderate quantities without growing ill. I do not see why this should be — water, to my mind, is water, and apparently even humans and elves need it now and again to survive — but I feel for her plight. As our stored water supplies are also quickly diminishing and there has been no rain in weeks,

Captain Vine instead grimaces and bears the aftertaste for the rest of the day.

My stomach still growls afterward, as the small ball of muck does little to assuage my hunger, but Captain Vine assures me that what it lacks in taste and substance, it makes up for in nutrition. All I can say is that it had better, because nothing short of malnourishment will ever make me put that back in my mouth again.

Needless to say, with the increasing severity of our food shortage, the unpleasantness of the slimeroot, and then my Captain's growing issue with thirst that the entirety of the sea around us is powerless to quench, our moods start to dampen. We become gloomy, anxious, our stomachs holding more frequent conversations than ourselves. My Captain stops making attempts to grope me or force a kiss; and while I realize that, on some strange level, I miss this behavior, I myself am too disparagingly miserable to do anything about it or even care.

Two days after the slimeroot, just as I am contemplating diving overboard to see if below the waves will be any kinder to me than atop them, we finally come within sight of the coast — a solid line of land stretching endlessly out before us, from one side of the horizon to the other. It is my first time seeing so much of it in one place, and as its arrival heralds an inevitable end to our growing misery, the sight cheers us both substantially — so much so that Vine throws herself at me for the first time in days, and I do not even make the pretense of resisting.

At first.

“Ah!” I gasp in surprise when her grip on my shoulder flashes sudden pain through my skin. I flinch back out of her grasp, and where her fingers drag across my flesh feels like a week-old jellyfish sting. I wince and raise my hands tentatively to my shoulders, checking for wounds.

“Lorelei,” my Captain says, surprised but less so than me, “you’re redder than a fox’s backside.”

“What?” I reply, looking up at her. “What does that mean?”

She frowns full of pity and steps closer again, gently laying her hands on the tops of my arms. Her skin feels mercifully cool, but my own where she touches throbs with a dull ache. “You’re sunburned,” she says, looking me over. “Like, kind of a lot.”

“Sun … burned?” I repeat, glancing up at the sky. The sun is directly above us, and while I know better than to look straight at it, even focusing on the cloudless blue dome around it hurts my eyes after a moment with its brightness. “But, how? I’ve not even touched the sun!”

Captain Vine laughs at that, one of her tinkling chuckles that mean I have said something to show my ignorance which she finds amusing. It’s been a while, I realize, since I last merited that reaction from her. “No, Lorelei, but it’s touched you. Or it might be more accurate to say that it’s reached down and smacked you around for a bit; you’ve got it worse than I’ve seen in years.”

I glare at her. My mood had already been low, and now her jesting at my pain is annoying me more than usual. “Then what must I do to fix it?” I demand.

Her smile calms and she shakes her head in pity. “I had medicine, but they took it. So all you can do now is wait it out ’til we find a town, then see if there’s a healer or apothecary that can help.” She steps forward and embraces me again, lightly this time, and in my waning irritation I allow it. “Sorry, babe. I should have realized sooner that you’d be a prime target with that milky-white skin. Can’t build up a tolerance underwater, can you?”

“How can something so far away hurt me just by illuminating me?” I gripe. “This is ludicrous.”

With the side of her head pressed to mine and her face safely out of sight, Captain Vine makes a sound in her throat as if she had made to laugh but thought better of it at the last moment. Then she releases me and, with her hands on my bottom (a place that has apparently been left mercifully undamaged), pushes me toward the cabin door. “Inside with you,” she commands. “Find a cozy dark cranny to rest in, it’ll make you feel better. I’ll find us a port before cabin fever strikes, promise.”

“Cabin — ?” I halt halfway through the door and whirl around back to her. “Is there *really* an affliction gained from remaining indoors? As well as one for remaining out of them?”

“Well, that was mostly a joke,” my Captain replies with a tilt of her head. “But, yes, that’s also a thing. I think I may have had it when we met, actually. One of the reasons I picked you up.”

I shake my head at this newfound knowledge. “Am I going to turn into you if I stay on this ship much longer?” That was probably part joke as well, but under this is real growing concern with what other strange surface ailments might be lurking around unbeknownst to me.

Captain Vine grins. "Maybe if you're lucky. You're already working on your first tan."

***

Thanks be to any gods listening that we eventually find a port later in the same day. I am sitting against the wall on the bed in the cabin, glaring out the porthole at the waning light of the traitorous sun as it paints the blue sky with the first hints of orange, when I hear a loud *whoop* from out on the deck, followed shortly by Captain Vine throwing the door open and leaning into the room, both hands gripping the doorframe, and wearing the biggest smile I've seen in days. "Lorelei!" she cries in excitement. "Port town! And it's got a forest!" She lets go of the doorframe then and throws herself into the room, twisting in midair to land with a thump on her back on the mattress with enough force to bounce me aside and send me toppling into the pillow. "A real forest, with, with trees and everything! Woo!"

I raise myself back up with a grateful sigh, already feeling my tension from the past couple of days starting to drain with the imminent promise of relief. If I do not have the energy or the inclination for my Captain's excitement, still I share the sentiment completely. "At last," I say, leaning my head back against the wall. "I do not know which I would prefer first: a full meal, or tending to this irritable burn."

"Food first," my Captain declares. She lifts her legs in the air and rolls them back, planting her feet against the wall over her head and staring up at the ceiling through her legs. "A meal for the both of us, then some light medical attention, then we'll see about getting the ship provisioned. Then we'll weigh what we've got left against what we need for repairs and think of a way to shore up the balance. And somewhere in there we'll go clothes shopping if you like, though we shouldn't need much in that respect seeing as how we only ever get dressed to go out in public."

She takes her feet from the wall then, stretches her legs high into the air, then flops them sprawling back to the mattress, which is when I realize that I've been staring at them. Of all her many toned and shapely parts, these are the two I have the hardest time getting over — no doubt mainly because of their exoticness when compared to the usual company I've kept all my life, as well as their graceful contrast to my own clumsy appendages. *Someday,* I tell myself silently, though honestly at this point I would be happy enough if I could simply walk a firm path without having to glance down at my feet every few seconds.

"And the forest!" she continues, audible awe in her tone. "We'll hafta check it out first, but we can probably get a lot of our groceries from there. Maybe find a nice private nook out of the elements and go camping. Oh, wouldn't that be fun, Lei?" She turns her bright eyes and brighter smile on me and bounces on her back on the mattress like an excited child.

"I'm sorry," I answer, "I do not know that I fully understand why a forest should be cause for such excitement. And what is camping?"

"Oohh, right," she says, sitting up. "You probably don't even know what a forest is, do you? Forgot for a sec."

"Of course I know of forests," I complain, and it is partially still the pain and hunger's fault that it comes out so snappy. "I am not *completely* ignorant, Captain, no matter how I may seem to you."

"Rowr," she says as she stands, and the meaning of the sound is completely lost on me. "You get kinda touchy when you're hungry, huh? And not in the fun way." Then her smile flashes back across her face like a barracuda on the hunt. "I'm gonna pull her into the dock here before much longer. If I tell the sun to back off, will you grace me with your presence at the helm?" She crosses one leg in front of the other, then bends low at the waist with one arm extended to her side. From the slow mechanics of it, this is evidently some kind of formal gesture. Which means she is probably mocking me again.

Still, I do feel a bit of guilt over being such unpleasant company of late. I stand, sigh, then mimic her gesture to the best of my ability, rising with my best haughty smile. "Very well, good Captain Vineberry," I reply, proffering my hand to her. "You may escort your princess to the deck."

Gently and gracefully, she takes my hand in hers and leads me like a true gentlewoman from the bedroom. And to her credit, we make it all the way to the cabin door before she bursts out giggling and rearranges our hands to places less dignified.

***

Captain Vine sets our course toward the small harbor, and we duck back into the cabin to put our clothes back on while the ship steers itself toward the dock. I still do not know how *The Queen's Runner* can do this, but apparently this singular quality is the main reason that my Captain can handle the ship as well as she does.

"I'd actually probably make a terrible sailor on a normal ship," she confides in me as she slides her feet into her knee-high boots. "Normal ships don't go where you want them to without the right wind hitting the right sails, and you need a team of people messing with the rigging and stuff like that all the time to make that happen. I assume," she adds. "Never been on any other ships, really."

"But I've seen you in the rigging," I say, slipping into my strapless sundress. The light fabric is thankfully merciful with my angry skin. "And you always look like you're dutifully doing … something."

"Oh, I know a bit," she says, wrapping her breasts in their red cotton top. "Trial and error, and if you look at it long enough you start to get an idea of why one thing ties to another. I try to do as much as I can the honest way, then let the magic make up for the rest."

"But why bother at all if the ship doesn't need it?"

"It still helps. And I try to just nudge her in the direction I need rather than shove her along." She reaches into her now bound-up cleavage and slips the wooden talisman out from between her breasts, holding it lightly but reverently in front of her on its cord. "It's not *my* magic moving her, see. I can't be sure it won't run out someday, so I try to conserve it as much as possible."

So her necklace *is* connected to the ship somehow. I had begun to suspect as much; that would explain why she wears it even when she wears nothing else, and how she brought *The Queen's Runner* to us on the prison docks of Rockquay when it had been sitting halfway across the city in the main harbor. Her constant care with it would be well spent if it is indeed the only means by which she can keep control of her own ship.

"You cannot tell if it will suddenly cease functioning?" I ask. "Why not?"

Her grip on the trinket tightens, and she shuts her eyes with a soft smile. "She never got the chance to explain it to me. That I made it this far on my own already is something of a personal miracle."

"She?" I repeat. "Who is 'she?'"

My Captain doesn't answer. I wonder if she realizes when she lapses into conversations that only she understands, or that she occasionally ignores my part of our discussions entirely. It could be that she is hesitant to share her history with me, but it is equally likely that she simply cannot be bothered to guide me along all of her meandering trains of thought, or else takes off down her own paths without bothering to see if I follow.

Regardless of her reasons, she simply tucks the talisman away in her chest again before heading back out on deck, and from there to the helm. I follow, reluctant to end the conversation now that I am finally getting something akin to personal reasoning out of her. "So if you cannot swim at all," I say, "and if you are a self-proclaimed terrible sailor, what are you doing out on the sea, sailing around on a ship powered by someone else's magic, all by yourself?"

Her smile dies out completely as she fixes a hard gaze on the approaching docks. "Lorelei," she says quietly, "what is the name of this ship again?"

"*The Queen's Runner?*" I answer, thrown off by the question.

"Exactly," she says, then pulls her bandana from her pocket and carefully ties back her hair to completely hide her pointed, elven ears. "And the farther you run, the harder it is to find your way home again." She takes a deep breath, holds it a moment, then lets it out slowly through her lips. "We'll be docked within the next ten minutes," she says to me, eyes still ahead. "Psyche yourself up if you haven't already."

It seems I have reached my limit for answers at the moment. "Yes, Captain."

***

The town, it turns out, is called Waterglade, and it is only about half the size of Rockquay with about a third of the population and none of the visitors besides ourselves. The harbor is made up of only four wharfs, one of which rests a ship half again as big as our own, two more crowded with a handful of smaller, simpler boats. The last sits empty, and we pull alongside it and tie on without any protest from the handful of men that watch our approach, though we do get plenty of curious stares — more so here than in Rockquay, where we were only one new arrival amongst many.

Captain Vine vaults purposefully from railing to pier and negotiates out of earshot with a couple of the watching men while I stumble my own way up to land. For some reason, as soon as I step off the ship, my legs feel as if they are newly grown once more, threatening to wobble out from under me and drop me to the planks beneath me. I am perplexed; I admit I am still far from mastering the limbs, but I know that I have gained a better proficiency with them than this. I had been striding around the deck of the ship with almost no issue just before docking, yet now I must trip my way to the nearest pole and lean against it while my forgetful feet sort themselves out.

"Sea legs," my Captain explains, amused, as she rejoins me. "The deck rocks with the tides, but dry land sits still and breaks them. But your legs haven't realized it yet, so they still wanna rock."

"I do not remember having this problem my first time on land," I complain, standing up straighter. True enough, my muscles try to tell me that they can feel the wood beneath me tilting back and forth, though I know them for liars.

"How would you have known?" my Captain giggles. "You were already falling on your ass every half dozen steps. You need to know how to walk first before you can know why you trip."

I reach out and clutch at her arm, steadying myself for the moment. "That's not funny," I accuse. *But, technically, it's true,* I silently admit.

"Don't worry," she says, grasping my elbow on the arm that holds her. "Happens to everyone their first few times. I'll make sure you don't embarrass yourself too badly before we get into town proper."

"Did it happen to you too?" I ask as we lurch our way up the beach.

"Oh, no, of course not," she says. "I've got the legs of a goddess and the grace of a deer in flight. Don't be ridiculous."

Sometimes I kind of hate her, just a little bit.

Waterglade, thankfully, is a much more open, less crowded place than Rockquay, with wide streets of packed dirt and stone and very few people moving along them. The docks we arrive in sit at the southern end of the town, the beach quickly sloping northward and giving way to solid earth covered in tiny blades of some sort of dry land-kelp. And further north, past the town and visible over the rooftops, is —

I stop in my wobbly tracks and gape. Looming over the town's edge and stretching away on either side, gigantic pieces of what looks like straight, brown coral stand tall as a whale is long, an uncountable number grouped as tightly as a school of herring, the whole mass blanketed on top by bushy mounds of some weed or algae. The sheer size and number of these growths astounds me. "What is all of that?" I ask my Captain.

She follows my line of sight to the school of coral and back, then quirks an eyebrow at me. "I thought you said you already knew what a forest was."

"Yes, but …" I shake my head. "Our forests do not look like *this*. And I had no idea coral grew on land as well."

"Coral?" my Captain repeats, looking away to the land forest again. "Those are trees, Lei. Living wood, like what the ship is made from."

"The ship is a kind of coral?" I ask. "Or part of a forest? Like a kelp?" I turn my confused gaze on my Captain. "*The Queen's Runner* is a vegetable?"

"Wha?" My Captain returns the look. "C'mon, Lei, you know what wood is by now, right? Seriously? This can't be new to you."

"I guess I simply never thought about where it originated," I answer as we resume our tandem walk into the heart of the town. "I mean, if ships are made from wood, and most land buildings are as well, I thought it would be more … I don't know, like some sort of ore?" I shrug. "It comes in so many shapes."

"You have to cut the trees into those shapes," Captain Vine explains, her tone like she's talking to a small and inquisitive child. She might as well be right now, I suppose, grating as the thought is. "Trees don't just grow into houses and ships naturally." She pauses thoughtfully, then shrugs. "Or at least they don't usually, and certainly not for humans. Now come on," she adds, tugging me along faster. "I'm as much of a tree hugger as the next elf, but they can wait. Food and a healer first, then we can go exploring the wilderness."

Food, thankfully, is easy to find, as vendors line the broadening street near the center of the town with open boxes of separated foodstuffs, all of it apparently for sale — green vegetables and multicolored fruits, hunks and strips of meat both raw and cooked in varying shades of red and brown, and the occasional collection of something that does not, to my eye, look edible at all, but must be if the knots of customers doing business over them are any indication. The crowds grow in the streets around this small marketplace, but they still do not reach Rockquay levels, and so even on my remedial legs I find I can manage to keep myself from being swept away or trampled over. Captain Vine takes us past several of these vendors, purchasing handfuls of fruits and vegetables for the both of us with some of the stolen coins in her pockets, and we sit to eat them near a hole in the ground ringed with a short stone wall in a nearby open plaza. Captain Vine hauls a bucket up from this hole on a rope attached to the stonework, then drinks deeply and thankfully from the clear water within. As no one passing by reprimands us for this, I assume it is expected and allowed, and so follow her example.

"At least our food resupply should be cheap with the forest so close by," my Captain remarks between bites of some crunchy, fist-sized thing with dark red skin and a white core. "If we have time, we can collect a good bit ourselves and save even more. The merchants here probably picked the obvious stuff clean, but there are always gifts to be had in the woods that you can count on humans to overlook."

I nod absently and eat faster, occasionally throwing wary glances at the sky in the direction of the sunset. Our situation at the moment is vastly improved to what it has been these past few days, but I find myself still leery of having no shade between myself and the open sky. I can feel my skin stretched uncomfortably tight with each movement of my limbs or twist of my torso.

Our meal finished and our stomachs satisfied for the first time in days, my Captain begins asking around for a healer. The few townsfolk she addresses point her in the same direction, but I notice that each makes a face before answering — a narrowing of the eyes or a slight frown, as though medicine were somehow distasteful to them. I do not know if my Captain notices this as well, and I do not bring it up for fear of voicing the obvious yet again and further showcasing my lack of experience with this world and these people.

The sun is hidden behind the buildings and steadily sinking to its destination beneath the ground when we find the place we're looking for at last — a small, square structure of faded gray-brown wooden boards with a ground and upper level, a sign of the same wood hanging over the front door that depicts a looping symbol curving in on itself that I do not recognize. Two windows face outward from the front, but one is covered by darker wooden boards nailed into the wall on either side, and the other holds a pane of glass with a jagged, violent hole in the center. My Captain frowns briefly at these before knocking twice on the closed door. When no answer seems forthcoming, she opens it and walks in, and I follow.

The entry room looks much like the merchant's shop we visited in Rockquay, where my Captain had thought to sell my discarded scales before events changed our plans. A wooden counter divides a far section of the room from the open area we stand in. Strewn across it and occupying shelves against the wall behind it are an assortment of dried plants tied in small bundles, stoppered jars with handwritten labels hiding their contents, and a handful of well-worn books and sheaves of paper. On our end of the room, a soft, warm oval of muted green cloth covers most of the floor, and padded seats with rests for the arms and back sit against the wall on either side of the front door. A stone alcove is built into the right side wall, though what its purpose is I do not know, and the left wall holds a mirror as tall as a grown man and twice as wide.

Captain Vine glances about the room, empty save for the two of us, then walks forward to lean on the counter and peer through the open doorway in the far wall. “Hello?” she calls. “Anybody home wanna heal some folks? Nothing too serious, we promise.”

“Sorry!” a voice calls from above and on the other side of the wall. “Just a moment, please!” This is followed by a cacophony of loud, rattling thumping noises, then one continuous thunking that starts at the back of the building above us and continues rhythmically down to our level. A moment later, a young woman about my size and height emerges from the back room, dragging a plank of wood about half as long as she is tall. “Sorry about that,” she says again, propping the board against the counter between her and us, then smiling brightly between my Captain and I. “Now, how may I help you?”

For a moment, I blink and stare and say nothing. My Captain has the same reaction, and I cannot blame her.

This woman is adorable. Her skin is a light shade of creamy brown, a bit lighter than Captain Vine’s, but with more softness and none of the angles. Golden hair frames her heart-shaped face and hangs down to the middle of her back, and large, dark brown eyes look us both over with a disarming warmth to them. I find myself inexplicably wanting to step around the counter and give her a hug, and the friendly smile on her face gives me the impression that the gesture would be allowed.

My Captain makes a quiet sound in her throat like she thinks the young woman in front of us looks tasty. I only notice because I have often heard her make that same sound at me right before intimate moments. For a second, I wonder if perhaps I should pull my Captain out of here before she does something improper; but she only smiles her disarming smile and puts an arm carefully around my stinging pink shoulders.

"We're sailors stopping over for some ship maintenance," she tells the adorable woman, "and while we're here, we figured we'd better get a bit ourselves. I got a couple of burns I'd like looked at, and my friend here lost an argument with the sun."

"I see," the adorable woman says, stepping around the counter to look us both over head-to-fin. Or head-to-toe, I suppose is the more accurate land term. I can't help but notice that her outfit is much nicer than anything my Captain or I have on — a fitted dress of the same light, bright green as the little weed blades that carpet the earth around the village, tapering to two loose points at her knees in the front and back. An arm's span of sheer white cloth with laced edges sits draped about her neck and shoulders, and a diamond-cut window in the front of her dress shows a decent amount of golden-tanned cleavage, though not so much as my Captain is fond of showcasing. I catch my eyes lingering there and quickly avert them. Unfortunately, as I seem to already be in that impolite mindset, I avert them down to her legs, the sides of which I can see peeking from her dress as far up as her mid-thighs. They are not Captain Vine's self-proclaimed goddess-like legs (a statement I find hard to form argument with), but still …

I forcibly avert my gaze upward this time, where it meets hers. She tilts her head thoughtfully as she searches my face. "You *are* pretty sunburned," she tells me. "Your face is especially red."

It grows redder still as I yank my gaze away from her a third time, embarrassed at myself for ogling a stranger. I catch my Captain's eyes this time, and from her smirk and the way she waggles her eyebrows at me, I can be sure that she knows the reaction I am having.

Gods below, perhaps I really *am* going to turn into her before long.

The woman steps closer to me then, reaching out to gently rest her fingertips on the outsides of my arms. They feel cool, slightly tingly, and as she drags them lightly up to my shoulders and then down the front of my arms, I shiver for the first time in what feels like a week. She nods with a frown, face full of concern. "It's widespread, to be sure," she says, "but not so very deep. I can set it right with little concern, don't worry." She smiles at me, then turns to my Captain. "May I see your injury as well?"

Still smirking knowingly at me in a way that makes me want to run away and check my ears for growing pointiness, she holds her wrists out to the woman, who gasps and brings her hand up against the bare skin of her chest peeking through the little window of her dress. "That bad?" Captain Vine asks, smile drooping.

"How did you …?" The healer woman trails off, then touches my Captain's burns as lightly as my own. Captain

Vine winces ever so slightly at the contact, but holds her arms steady as the woman prods gingerly and stares. When she looks up again, her brow is scrunched with worry. "How did you get this burn?" she asks my Captain.

Captain Vine shrugs. "I fumbled a torch across my arms. Clumsy, I know, but I was distracted."

"Hmm …" The woman's brow scrunches further as she turns her attention back to Vine's wrists. "That's not what it looks like. It looks almost like …" She steps back as she trails off again, then looks seriously into my Captain's eyes. "Ma'am," she says quietly, "forgive me if this seems a weird question, but … are you human?"

My breath catches in my throat at that, and I glance nervously at my Captain, hoping that this doesn't turn into a repeat of the disaster at Rockquay and that this nice, friendly healer woman won't suddenly call the authorities on us. My Captain glances back at me in wide-eyed panic for a moment before quickly turning her attention back to the healer. "What?" she asks, not needing to feign the surprise in her voice. "What kind of question is that? What else would I be?"

"I'm sorry if I offend, ma'am," the healer woman says with a bow of her head. "But I need to know for certain."

"Of course I am!" my Captain answers perhaps a bit too loudly. "What do I look like, a plucked chicken or something?"

"No, ma'am," the woman answers calmly. "But the damage on your arms doesn't resemble a normal burn. In fact, to be blunt, it looks remarkably similar to the kind of burn that iron induces in the fae folk."

Captain Vine blinks, gulps audibly, and says nothing. For my part, I'm suddenly grateful that the healer woman isn't looking at me right now, as I already know how abysmal I am at lying under pressure.

"Ma'am," the woman continues, "tell me the truth, please. Are you a fairy?" Her tone is serious, yet reassuring, as if she is patiently trying to persuade a small child to stop lying. Regardless, I can see my Captain shooting longing glances at the doorway. The healer must see it too, as she raises her hands as if to show that she poses no threat. "It's perfectly alright if you are," she says quietly. "I'm only asking so that I know how to go about healing your wounds. I promise you, I hold no fear or anger toward fae folk of any variety. You need fear no conflict by telling me the truth."

My Captain eyes the young woman in tense silence for several long seconds after that, the set of her frown making it obvious that she is still debating whether the truth or more lies is the best response, before finally taking a deep breath and releasing it slowly. "Well you truly don't know the fae if you think you don't fear or hate *any* of them," she mumbles at last, crossing her arms and turning her gaze to mirror on the side wall. "But … yes. Alright. I'm elven, if you must know."

The woman's smile returns, and she bows her head once more. "I'm afraid I must," she says. "But thank you for your honesty. I promise, your secret will be safe with me."

"Yeah, thanks," my Captain mumbles, her mirth still absent. But she holds her arms out again without reservation. "So, how bad is it?"

I release a deep breath of my own that I hadn't realized I'd been holding, my whole body relaxing as the tension leaves the room. Thankfully, despite my Captain's concerns and private warnings to me, what she is does not make her a pariah quite everywhere she goes.

The healer looks at her burns once more, turning her wrists over to examine them from every angle. "Bad," she says, "but not horrible. The damage is deeper than your friend, obviously, and more than you would get from momentary contact with fire. Thankfully, though, it doesn't eat so deep as to damage the nerves or deep muscle tissue." She looks up at my Captain then, and now it is her turn to look awkward and uncomfortable. "I can heal this. The treatment should only take a few minutes, but … my methods are a bit, um … unique." She glances my way as if seeking support, then back at Captain Vine. "I must ask your trust again, I'm afraid. I will need your cooperation to address your injuries properly."

My Captain quirks an eyebrow at the small woman. "What exactly do I have to do?"

"Um …"

The healer looks my way again, and this time I believe I can see a reddish tinge to the soft brown of her face. Is *she* blushing now, too? Why would she suddenly be embarrassed to do her job?

Before I can ask, she turns back to my Captain, eyes on the floor. "Perhaps it's best to simply do it quickly and not dwell on it. Give me your wrists, please," she says softly, and Captain Vine holds them out with understandable hesitancy. The healer lightly clasps them in her hands, fingers covering the whole burn area. "Now close your eyes," she commands, still not looking up.

Captain Vine, with one last confused look my way, closes her eyes. The healer takes a deep breath, then rises up on her toes and plants her lips firmly against my Captain's.

I gasp, stunned. This is the last thing I expected to happen, and evidently it takes my Captain by surprise too, as I see her body tense visibly, her hands clenching to fists in the healer's grasp. However, unlike me, Captain Vine's tension softens as quickly as it came, her hands relaxing as the young woman holds her arms, her face leaning down to deepen the surprise kiss. One of them, I'm not sure which, moans quietly into the other's mouth, and my Captain pulls away just enough that I can see her tongue is sliding over the healer's before their lips lock once more.

I am … unsure how to react, to put it lightly. On the one hand, watching these two relax into each other like this, I feel a familiar warm tingle that I haven't felt in days since we began going hungry on *The Queen's Runner.* This healer girl is about my size, I remember; this, then, must be what my Captain and I look like to outside observers when we kiss in this manner. And with the luxury of a third-party perspective, I can observe things in ways that I cannot when I am a participant swept up in the act — things like the relaxed longing on both of their faces as they surrender to each other, and the way my Captain's legs slide ever so subtly toward the girl in front of her as if to accommodate some new sensation spreading between them, and the quiet little wet sounds their mouths make against one another, and the way their breathing grows heavier in their chests, and how the bottom of my taller Captain's full breasts rest snugly against the exposed valley of the shorter woman's heaving —

I snap out of my thoughts when I realize that I've put my hand to my mouth and that my finger is subconsciously prodding at my lips. The other is slowly heading in a different direction that I quickly intercept, forcing them both down to my sides where they must behave themselves. I realize now that my Captain and I have done nothing like this with one another during these past several days while we desperately searched for somewhere to dock; several days without intimacy that I would not have thought to bemoan before coming to the surface, but which nevertheless represent the longest I have gone without it since meeting Captain Vine.

And now Captain Vine is giving that attention to this stranger, and I remember the other hand of my reaction.

It sounds ridiculous when I think of it in words like this — petulant almost, like a spoiled child not getting their way for once — but, well … I have come to think of my Captain as just that. *My* Captain. And while I know for a fact, even if she has not said so outright, that I am not the first person that she has behaved like this with, and probably not even the first other girl, still … to see it in person, with me standing right here, after everything we've done together … I feel sort of …

And that is when I notice that, beneath the healer's touch, Captain Vine's arms are glowing brightly along her burn marks, and a new shock replaces my initial one.

It is a minute longer before the light's radiance fades and the healer lowers herself to her feet once more, pulling her mouth away from my Captain's. She releases Vine's wrists and clasps her empty hands in front of her, looking down at her own feet, her now-obvious blush still there. My Captain lazily opens her eyes to find her wounds still glowing slightly, and she and I both stare in wonder at this until the light fades out completely, leaving unblemished bands of skin a few shades lighter than that around it where her slow-leaking wounds had been only minutes before.

In the still silence, the healer is the first to speak. “Sorry,” she whispers, not looking at either of us. “How do they look?”

In lieu of an answer, Captain Vine carefully pokes at the healed flesh of one wrist, then rubs it tenderly, turning her arm over to find only clean, healthy skin and no lingering traces of the burns left. She looks up at the healer with this same awed expression. “That was spirit magic, wasn’t it?” she asks quietly.

The young healer looks even more abashed than before if possible, but bobs her head in quick affirmation.

“I didn’t know humans had that,” my Captain continues, inspecting her healed skin with more gusto now. “Heck, I wasn’t even entirely sure humans had magic of any sort.”

“Most don’t,” the healer quietly explains. “Very few people are born with any sort of magical talent. Fewer still can work the spirit. But I can.” She finally hazards a glance at my Captain through her blush. “Sorry,” she says again.

“Why?” Captain Vine answers with a smile, flexing her wrists. “I feel great now. Why would you need to apologize for fixing me?” Her smile turns coy, and she leans in closer to the embarrassed girl. “Or are you apologizing for that kiss you stole?”

The healer sighs, yet strangely seems less flustered for the teasing. “The kiss helped me reach deeper into you to tap your spirit more strongly. Your burns were only skin deep, but ate deeply into your skin, beyond the effectiveness of surface redirection. I simply figured …" She trails off, averting her eyes once more. "Well … I figured, being fae, you wouldn't mind the breach of propriety or the use of magic as much as the average human would."

"I didn't," my Captain answers with a grin and a chuckle, looking the healer over in a manner hitherto reserved only for me. Then, as if remembering my presence, my Captain crosses the room to me and puts both of her hands on my shoulders, presenting me to the blushing woman as if she were about to barter me off. "I also don't mind if you need to make out with my mermaid to fix her too. Heal away." She flashes her grin at me, then steps back and crosses her arms beneath her breasts. "I'll watch."

"Mermaid?" the healer repeats, eyes going wide as they turn on me and drop to my bare legs.

My conflicting feelings from a moment ago are shuffled aside under this new scrutiny, and I tug the hem of my dress down further as my face reddens yet again. Is it now my turn to be so deeply and tenderly kissed by this attractive stranger? How many times in one life are beautiful women going to fondle me before I even know their names? The thought speeds up my heartbeat to the point that I can feel it thumping against my chest.

"Pretty, isn't she?" Captain Vine says, and it takes me a moment to realize that she is talking to the healer. About me. "Found her about a week south of here. Her name's Lorelei." She crosses her legs and sweeps her torso down in the same bowing gesture she showed me in our cabin before we docked. "And while we're on introductions, I'm Captain

Jerica Vine. Which, since you already know my guilty secret, you'll note is not my real name."

The woman smiles slightly at the both of us, bowing her head at first my Captain and then me. "I am Amarante. It is a pleasure to meet you, Captain Vine, Lorelei."

"A pleasure," I murmur as I stare at my feet, all my many years of etiquette and politesse momentarily useless.

Because of or in spite of my embarrassment, my Captain chooses this moment to drape her arm across my shoulders again and smirk. "Don't be fooled by her proper and shy routine," she confides in the healer. "Beneath that innocent mien, she's completely insatiable." And she punctuates this statement by giving my breast a light, quick squeeze through my dress in plain view of Amarante.

"Captain!" I gasp in horror, pushing her back off of me and shutting my eyes tight against the heat rushing to my face, which I am certain is red as my hair by now. I wish with no little sincerity that the ground might open beneath my feet and swallow me whole very soon.

Amarante, thankfully, either does not catch on to my Captain's mockery or simply chooses to ignore it. "Are you really a mermaid?" she asks me in awe, looking me over in a completely different way than my Captain usually does. "That's incredible! Oh, I mean," she adds quickly, hand flying to her bare window of chest, "not to imply that you're some strange creature or anything. Sorry. It's just … well, I didn't even know that your kind were real." She smiles apologetically at me, the fascination clear on her face, and I find her open friendliness too great to feel any resentment for her attention toward either me or my Captain.

"She's real," Captain Vine chimes in. "Feel her."

Captain Vine is not receiving the same pardon right now.

"I apologize if I seem overenthusiastic," Amarante continues, her continued lack of acknowledgment toward my Captain's goading only endearing her further to me. "I had heard stories of merfolk as a child, but this is my first time meeting one. I think." She pauses a moment, brow furrowed in thought, before smiling brightly. "Perhaps not, though," she continues. "If you can form legs and walk amongst us on land, perhaps I've already met a dozen. But I can't say I have ever knowingly healed one." She bows her head at me again, hands clasped before her. "I am sorry. I will try my best, though. I believe my methods should work regardless, but one never knows."

Her methods. I gulp. "Must we … I mean, are you going to …?" I mutter. My hands fidget with my dress, and as I cannot think of a better application for them, I do not stop them.

"Do we have to kiss for me to heal you?" she asks for me with a smile, then shakes her head. "No, not for a sunburn. It only touches the surface; I can make do with the edge of your life-force."

"Aww," pouts my Captain. I manage a glare out the corner of my eyes in her general direction.

"I only need access to the full afflicted area," Amarante continues, stepping closer to me and laying her hands gently on my sun baked arms. "I'm assuming the damage stops at the edges of your outfit?"

“Oh. Um, no,” I answer, looking myself over along with her. “The sun damage seems to have occurred over most of my body, actually.”

“Oh. I see.” She steps back and clears her throat. “Then you will need to remove your dress for me, please.”

I blink at her for a moment before her words register. “I must be naked?” I ask, though I do not know why I do; her meaning was clear enough the first time. And honestly, disrobing for her should not bother me — I did not even *wear* clothes before coming to the surface, only shells to cover my breasts, which back then were the start and finish of the thoughts I had ever given toward modesty. This dress I wear, my only garment, was my Captain’s idea, a practice she ensured me was necessary to the etiquette of human culture. But for that I would not have thought to wear anything, and indeed have always been comfortable in my nudity before without thinking to question it.

But I have been conditioned these short few weeks, it seems, to view clothing as a new necessity to public dignity. It does not help that I am only ever truly without it when I am alone with Captain Vine, when dignity is no longer a concern nor even an option. I have come to view the baring of my body as a prelude to private intimacy, my naked flesh full of potential I had never given thought to before.

Now I was being asked to bare myself before another woman I have only just met, who has already been making me question the exclusivity of that same intimacy to which my Captain has introduced me. I hesitate, no longer sure where the bounds of modesty lie.

Amarante watches my face as all of this goes through my head, then giggles lightly. "I think you may be over thinking this," she tells me quietly, then glances toward Captain Vine. "If you prefer, we can take this in back and do it in private, if it makes you more comfortable."

I follow her gaze to my Captain, who quirks an eyebrow at the both of us as if wondering what she has to do with anything. In truth, *her* seeing me naked was my last concern — worrying about my modesty in front of her now would mean backing up to a past lifetime. But as I think about it …

"Yes, please" I say, turning back to the healer. "I think I would like that."

As expected, Captain Vine's brow furrows, a look of sudden disappointment wiping away her smile. "Aww," she pouts, "no fair. I showed you mine."

"We will only be a moment, I assure you," Amarante says to her, taking my arm lightly in her hand and turning me toward the back doorway. "Please, have a seat, make yourself at home." With a last polite smile to my frowning Captain, she turns us both away and leads me through the doorway. I hear Captain Vine flop dejectedly onto one of the padded seats as I pass into the next room behind the counter.

It resembles a storeroom, but larger. More shelves line the walls, more books and jars and small plants filling them, and every other surface including the floor is covered in papers and books of all sizes. Against the wall and extruding outward from it is a series of raised platforms, each higher than the last in the same regular intervals. I stop and watch a moment as Amarante climbs these one foot at a time, each step taking her higher up until she passes through a hole in the ceiling. Intrigued by the simplicity of this construction, I follow her example, steadying myself on the wall with one hand as I go. It is not unlike climbing a hill, yet somehow easier for the level steps. I had assumed until now that humans climbed to higher rooms in their dwellings the same way my Captain climbs the rigging of her ship, but this system seems much more practical.

She smiles at me when I reach the top. She smiles almost as much as Captain Vine, it seems, but without the mischief. "You really are a mermaid," she says. "You seem so unsure of your legs, and you climb stairs like you've never seen them before."

"I haven't," I say, turning to look down at the floor far below me. "What did you call them? 'Stairs?'"

She giggles again, then leads me past a haphazard pile of differently sized wooden planks like the one she'd drug into the front room with her when she met us. I suddenly realize what all the commotion was that we'd heard on our arrival. "Pardon my mess, please," she says as we pass through another nearby doorway into what looks like a small bedroom. "I, uh, had a surprise repair project thrust upon me recently, and my organization's suffered as I try to figure out how to go about it."

"You mean your broken front window?" I ask, looking around this new room. It's small, smaller even than the storage-looking room with the stairs. The roof slants down from the inner wall to the outside wall, meaning the ceiling is several feet above my head near the door and several inches below it at the window. The only furnishings are a small bed in the corner, barely big enough for one person and made of roughly carved wood, and a small chest in the far opposite corner of the same simple construction, closed but without a lock. The room's only window lets in the last of the sunset's smoldering light, bathing us both in orange and accentuating my already red skin.

"Yes," she says, then sighs. "It's the second one this month. I should know by now not to bother replacing the glass."

"Did something bad happen?" I ask. "Was there a storm, or …?"

"This time? There was a brick." She shakes her head as if the event was to be expected and isn't worth discussing. "Now, if you'll please, I need to see the full burn."

My blush comes back at that. Now that it's just the two of us, I think I might have preferred my Captain's presence after all — uncouth though she may be at times, at least hers is an attention I am used to, and her teasing does strangely seem to make light of any embarrassment happening around her regardless of who it belongs to, as if shame were a concept with which she personally disagrees and cannot understand why anyone would take up. Nevertheless, I have made my decision, and I know I have nothing to fear from this woman; and so, eyes downcast and unable to stem the tide of color to my face, I wrap my arms about myself and grasp my dress in both hands, tugging it gently downward until it drops of its own accord to pool about my feet. My sunburn extends the full length of my upper body, mercifully dying out around my hips to leave everything between my waist and my thighs its usual unblemished, pale pink before taking up again at my knees to burn my lower legs down to my toes.

Amarante steps closer, a thoughtful noise in her throat. I risk a glance up. She has a finger on her chin and looks me up and down, a slight frown on her lips. The look on her face is the same detached, professional concern she had been showing me before I disrobed, and this lack of a change in her demeanor helps to lighten my shyness.

She steps behind me, lightly touching my shoulder, her fingers strangely refreshing against my skin. I sigh and lean into her touch before I think to wonder if the motion would be appropriate. "It's not bad," she says softly behind me, "but it's extensive. I'll need to draw your energy to the top in thin, wide waves."

I do not know what this means or what it entails. "Very well," I assure her. "Please do whatever you must." I expect to feel her hands caressing my back, healing with her touch the way she did with Captain Vine's wrists.

And indeed, after a few seconds wait and some light rustling behind me, I feel her hands lightly grip my shoulders, then slide gently down my upper arms. Her touch leaves cool lines of soothing relief on my flesh, and I shudder pleasantly as the pain and tightness melt away, replaced by a tingling chill. It is as if I had been sunning myself on a hot shoal for hours before slipping gently back into cool, deep water. For the first time in several days, I feel completely relaxed.

So lost am I in the pleasant sensation that, when I feel it spread suddenly to my upper back, it is all I can do to remain standing and not sink back into it. My eyes slip closed, my head lulls forward, and I relish the sensation for several long, delightful moments before I stop to wonder about it. Her hands are still gently stroking my arms. I can feel the soothing healing ripple outward slightly from her palms, but it doesn't spread across my body without her touch. So where is my back feeling it from?

Then she steps closer to me still, her fingers trailing down my forearms to clasp my wrists, and in the motion I feel her body squish firmer against my own. The source of the feeling on my back I now recognize as her breasts, the feeling spreading wider still as she presses them to me. Her stomach brushes my lower back, sending a brief tingle of relief through it, and where her arms slide along mine likewise sooths.

She is using her whole body as a healing conduit, not just her hands. Which means that, behind me, she is as naked as I am.

"You're tensing," she says quietly into my ear, her breath warm on my neck. "I understand. But I would like you to please trust me, if you can. It will be more effective if you stay relaxed."

I do not think I can at first. But as her hands slip from my wrists to my stomach, as the front of her body gently shifts against the back of mine, the soothing ripples of healing comfort overpower my tension. As with my Captain, her touch simply feels too good to resist. But where my Captain's touch heats me up and makes me squirm, the healer's cools me down and lulls my body to relaxed stillness. My breathing deepens the longer her touch lingers. I do not even care when her hands slip up my stomach to my chest, cupping each pink, sun-damaged breast in a soft hold and slowly caressing the discomfort from them. My head finally does loll back then, resting between her neck and shoulder, her golden hair brushing over my ruby hair and tickling my face. She laughs at this — not the throaty, hungry chuckle of my Captain when she likewise holds me, but a light, amused giggle.

I am not sure when we move to the bed. I don't remember making the transition myself. But soon I am lying on my back on top of the blanket, one leg lifted slightly for Amarante, who kneels beside me and slides her arms along it. My skin here, red-pink like a starfish, gives way to its usual pinkish white as her fingers move along it, the points of contact glowing gently as she massages away the damage.

"It's still a bit strange to me, a mermaid with legs," she says quietly with a smile as she rubs them down. "They're very nice for being new, though. And you handle yourself well on them. I never would have guessed on my own."

I think I can forgive Captain Vine now for kissing this woman so passionately in front of me. I want to do so myself right about now.

When she is done with my legs, I turn over for her on the bed. She bundles my hair to the side of my neck, clearing it from my shoulders, and lies atop me, her naked front against my naked back once more. I close my eyes in pure comfort, but not before I catch a glimpse of the soft glow between us, gently illuminating her brown skin against my white. I am not quite so pale as I was before this, I think — some of the sun's presence yet lingers on my body even as the worst of it melts away beneath her. I wonder, idly, how long she and my Captain must have spent in the sun to acquire the skin tones they have now, or if perhaps they were simply born that dusky.

Her hands continue to caress my sides, her legs intertwined with mine, her bosom slipping up and down my back and shoulder blades with the slow regularity of the sea lapping at the coast. I sigh deeply, contentedly, eyes still shut, losing myself in the sensation of this long, extended moment. I no longer have the will to think of anything else.

"You're not tense at all anymore," she says very quietly above me. "I'm glad. How does it feel now?"

I drift off before I can answer her.

***

The soft murmur of nearby voices eventually draws me back to waking. I sit up in bed, momentarily disoriented, and rub the sleep from my eyes. Someone had drawn a blanket over my naked body while I slept, which now falls away. Moonlight spills in from the room's only window, on the short wall at the end of the ceiling's slant, and casts the sparse furnishings in silver shadows. A brighter, flickering orange light peeks in around the door, through which a conversation that I can barely make out filters. I slide my legs out of bed, marveling at how much more pleasant my own skin feels to me now, and stand with a stretch and a yawn. Then I walk quietly to the doorway and open it just a crack.

"… need to keep an eye on my ship, but I don't wanna leave her here alone," Captain Vine's voice says quietly from the other room. I can barely make out her silhouette through the crack in the door, backlit by the flickering light that I now recognize as a sort of small fire. She is standing by the top of the staircase, her back to me, talking to Amarante. The healer seems to be holding the small fire in her hand somehow, the light carving her face from the shadows around them. I remember my Captain mentioning how putting one's hand in a fire was considered supremely painful, and I wonder briefly how this healer manages to do just that before my attention turns back to their conversation.

"I can assure you the docks are completely safe," Amarante answers my Captain just as quietly. "Waterglade has little security, but almost all of it is centered on the harbor. But if you are truly concerned, you can return if you like. I can watch over her for tonight."

"Thanks," my Captain replies, and I can hear that easy laugh of hers in her voice as she does so. "And it's not that I don't trust you, but … well …" Her hand comes up to rub the back of her neck, and she turns to glance back toward my door. She must not notice me, however, because she continues as if I weren't there. "She's still new to just about everything, and her introduction to land life wasn't exactly smooth. And I'm not sure where we stand with each other right now. If she woke up in a strange place and I wasn't there … I just don't want it to seem like I'm abandoning her." She sighs. "I dunno. It just makes me uncomfortable, for some reason. Maybe I'm just being possessive."

"You care for her," Amarante says with a visible smile. "That's understandable. And whatever my reassurances, I am still a stranger to you two. You're not offending me by not trusting me completely with your safety."

"Thanks," my Captain repeats. "You can add a room charge to our bill if you like. Only seems fair."

"Um, well, you can give me some money for staying the night if you like," Amarante says, her smile wilting, "but there's no charge for the healing."

"That's really nice of you," Captain Vine says, "but you don't have to make an exception for us. You've been nice enough already, and much as I prefer having money to not having it, I don't want you to think we're taking advantage of you."

"Oh, no, it's not an exception," the healer replies with a shake of her head. "I simply don't charge for those services. To anyone."

The silhouette of my Captain's head tilts. "You don't charge for healing? Is this a charity?"

"It sort of is. I can't charge for performing magic. It's not allowed. I just do that part to help people."

"Magic is illegal here?" my Captain asks, sounding more disbelieving with each word.

"Profiting from it is, yes," says Amarante. "Across the whole United Freelands. Practicing magic itself is legal, just … not encouraged," she finishes with a mumble, hanging her head.

There is a moment of silence between them as Captain Vine looks toward the pile of wooden planks and Amarante simply looks disappointed. "Those windows were vandalism," my Captain says. "And from the supplies you've got up here, it happens a lot, doesn't it?" She looks back to the healer, all humor gone from her tone. "The people here hate your being a mage, and you put up with it and help them anyway."

"Most people don't hate me personally," Amarante answers, sounding tired. "But magic is rare in humans, and how it manifests from one person to another varies wildly and without much pattern. People fear it. It's an uncertainty, one that gives them a disadvantage over whoever has it. Mages are more dangerous than most."

"Some, maybe. But how is spirit magic gonna threaten them? You might heal their wounds when they're not looking or something?"

"It has its own dangers. Healing is the obvious route, but it's done by manipulating life energy. I hold your health in my hand when I work. That doesn't necessarily mean I have to be kind to it." She holds her empty hand palm-up between them, staring at it as if it were a dangerous animal she dare not take her eyes off of. "I can manipulate your spirit the same way you would manipulate a bit of rope. I can unwind it from where it is and loop it about other places, redirect it. Change the flow. I use this talent to heal. But that isn't my only option." She closes her eyes as if ashamed, cupping both of her hands around the flame she holds. "If I wanted, I could direct your life flow to places it did not need to be, away from places it does. I could make it waste itself. Dam it up. I could make you sick this way, or infirm, or disable your limbs, your organs, your mind. Or I could simply spill it into the ground beneath you and kill you. If I so chose."

My Captain takes a step back at that. I myself notice that I am now gripping the wood of the door harder than necessary and have not blinked for longer than normal. Amarante makes no acknowledgement of either of us.

"I do not choose," she continues quietly after a pause, "but who's to say I might not later, in other circumstances? Who can say I will not become so angry with a patient some day that I destroy his health in a fit of pique? I do not think I would ever do that, but I cannot be entirely sure myself. People who know me less than I do certainly cannot be sure enough to risk themselves entirely." She opens her eyes then, looking steadily at my Captain, her expression stern. "I have greater potential for harm than the average individual, as well as greater potential for good, because of my talent. That is why I am feared despite my charity. That is why I am watched and judged at all times, even if I am occasionally judged unfairly. Because it is necessary. Because I am the last person in this village that can afford to deviate." There is a tense pause of a moment, and then Amarante smiles very slightly, very politely, at Captain Vine. "That is also why I don't blame you for not trusting me entirely with your companion's safety after we've just met. No one else does either. I understand."

My Captain's head turns back to my doorway, her face still shrouded in shadow. Again she seems not to notice me before turning back to Amarante. "Do you really believe all that," she asks the healer, "or does repeating that mantra just make you think that you do?"

Amarante giggles, the sound strange after the gravity of the recent moment. "I used to share your skepticism," she tells my Captain. "When I was a girl, I was angry with the unequal treatment that I and other mages received. But I have seen enough of magic and of the common people to understand it. You ask if I believe it?" She takes a deep breath and lets it out as a prolonged sigh. “I do. It saddens me at times, I admit, but I do believe in it. And within these boundaries, I have learned to live happily.”

Captain Vine’s head droops, and I get the impression that she has her face in her hands. “I will never understand you people,” she mutters.

Amarante giggles again, soft and light. “I imagine many aspects of humans must seem strange next to the carefree fae folk.”

“Something like that,” my Captain mumbles, and her voice seems sadder than usual again. “I’m going to bed now. If you don’t mind boarding us.”

“As I said, not at all,” replies the healer, moving toward the stairs with her little portable fire. “Please let me know if you require anything else. Goodnight, Captain Vine.”

My Captain says nothing as Amarante descends to the lower floor of the building, taking the light with her and leaving the scene outside my door steeped in darkness. I step back from the door, the light of the moon spilling around my shadow the only illumination left, and I am still readjusting to it when the door opens and my Captain walks in, directly up to me, and wraps her arms around me as if expecting me to be standing there all along. “How long were you spying on us?” she asks quietly, and once more I can hear her smile in her voice.

“Not long,” I admit, wrapping my arms around her as well. “I thought that fire was not to be touched. How is it that she could hold it in her hand so without issue? More magic?”

“Magic could probably do that, yes,” my Captain answers. “It’s easier to just use a candle, though.”

Her answer means nothing to me, which I suspect she already knows.

"Is she wrong, Lorelei?" Captain Vine asks next, now sounding troubled. "Or am I? How much of your freedom do you owe to people's peace of mind?"

"Captain?" I look for her face in the darkness but cannot make out its details. "Do you ask me about civic duty, or is this some deeper philosophy?"

"Neither," she says. "Nevermind. I don't want to talk about it after all." Her fingers slide through my hair, her lips press softly against my forehead. "I just want to take my mermaid and go to bed."

I smile against her skin. "Your mermaid would like that, Captain."

We fall asleep tangled in one another on the narrow bed, my body draped over hers, her arms lying across my back, both of my legs intertwined with her perfect ones. With my face nuzzled in the crook of her neck, I can feel each deep breath as she drifts off, smell the warm breeze in her hair. Her presence lulls me to sleep like a familiar lullaby.

It is nice. If I had been angry with her earlier today, I am not any longer. I feel only contentment.

***

The next morning, we come downstairs together to find that Amarante has prepared breakfast for the three of us. There are oblong chunks of some brown, sponge-like substance with jars of glistening purple goo that is sticky to the touch, along with what look like small, self-contained puddles of white with quivering yellow centers.

I do not wish to appear out of my depth anymore than I can help, but this land food is once again new to me. I had thought I'd been doing well to finally learn the names of most of the fruits and vegetables that my Captain and I had been eating, but none of the spread before us resembles a plant. I pick up the spongy brown lump and squeeze it experimentally before taking a cautious bite.

It tastes like nothing very much, which is more than I had hoped. It does dry my mouth out somewhat eating it, but I can manage.

My Captain is showing even less enthusiasm for her meal than myself, leaning her elbows on the table and resting her face in her hands. "Hey," she says offhandedly to Amarante, "sorry for the trust issues yesterday. I don't think I apologized for that, but it seems like something where I should."

"Think nothing of it," Amarante answers with an easy smile, dipping a small knife into the jar of purple goop. She brings it out laden with a jiggling dollop of the stuff and begins smearing it in a fine coating across her own brown sponge. "It's completely understandable why you'd be cautious of your heritage," she says to Captain Vine as she does this. "In fact, though it saddens me to say this, I would keep hiding it if I were you if you plan on being in this town for a while."

"Don't worry, I have every intention to," my Captain answers, pushing her food around her plate with her fork. "I gave up a long time ago expecting everybody to be as relaxed about it as you are."

"Yes, I'm afraid our villagers are not the most open-minded," Amarante says with a sigh. "Especially with the recent trouble."

"Trouble?" My Captain looks up from her plate, looking interested in the present finally.

"Oh, it's nothing to concern yourself about now, I'm sure," the healer answers with a shake of her head as she passes the jar of purple goo to me with the knife still in it. "But a few days ago, another fae wandered through our town. Another elf, actually. I didn't get a look at him myself, but I treated most of his victims."

Despite Amarante's reassurance, I can see Captain Vine suddenly stiffen with concern. Truth be told, I share it myself somewhat. Our last town was volatile enough with an elf who wanted no trouble from anyone. How much worse could this one potentially be after an elf passed through causing deliberate damage?

"What happened?" my Captain asks cautiously. No doubt her thoughts closely mirror my own about now.

Amarante sighs, staring down at her plate with the brown sponge in her hand. "He was involved in a rather large brawl at the village tavern," she explains. "The locals all say that he started it, but I don't know how much I believe them. All I know is he apparently made no effort to hide that he was not human, and he must have been an expert swordsman." She sets her sponge back down on her plate untasted, takes a sip of water, and shakes her head again as she continues. "It sounds like nearly the entire tavern ganged up on him that night after the commotion started in earnest. Somehow, though, he managed to get away, and those he left behind were all the worse off for it." She goes quiet for a moment, staring off through the distance. "Many I couldn't help," she says even more quietly, her voice somber. "They either died instantly or bled out before I could attend to them."

In the stifled atmosphere that follows, Captain Vine looks at me across the table. I can see the concern clearly in her eyes. She wants to finish our business and move on to another town as soon as possible. I nod at the unspoken question, and she looks back to Amarante. "I'm sorry to hear that," she says, though whether she is sorry most for the healer's plight or our own predicament, I cannot tell. "We'll be sure not to cause trouble unduly, don't worry."

Amarante smiles softly at my Captain and picks up her goo-covered sponge again. "I know you won't," she says. "Whatever species you two may be, I can tell that you're good people."

"Well, good enough, anyway," says Captain Vine, turning her attention back to her food but still not eating any. "We'll be done and gone even quicker if you can point us to a few places around town."

"Of course," says Amarante. "Where did you need to go?"

With the conversation taking a lighter path, I turn my attention to my own food as well. As casually as I can manage, as if I have eaten this meal many a time before already, I take the jar of purple goo with the knife in it and mimic our hostess. It takes a bit of maneuvering, but I succeed in wrestling a glob of the glistening purple goop onto my brown spongy thing and set about spreading it around.

"In no particular order of importance," I hear my Captain say, "we need a clothier and some cheap ship repair services.

And we're gonna need to resupply. Food stores, canvas, rope, that sorta thing."

Amarante makes a thoughtful noise as she cuts into one of the white and yellow puddles with her fork, setting the yellow bit free to ooze slowly across her plate. "I can point you to our tailor and our ship supply depot, but I'm afraid the only repairmen you'll find for your ship around here won't come cheap. Everyone pretty much does their own maintenance on their own vessels, so they tend to make repairs for travelers well worth the demand on their time." She stabs a slice of her oozing puddle then with her fork and pops it into her mouth.

I make a mental note of it as I finish up with my goo smearing project.

My Captain groans and hangs her head. "Figured as much," she mumbles. "Then we're gonna need to find a way to raise some money in a hurry while we're here, because we won't be getting much farther on the *Runner* with her like she is now."

I frown in sympathy with Captain Vine, then finally take my second bite of the now goo-slathered sponge. It is now the single sweetest thing that I have ever tasted in my life thus far, and I am somewhat embarrassed to say that my eyes rolled upward slightly of their own accord. I sit back and chew slowly, savoring the flavor until I notice that my Captain is looking directly at me again.

I stop chewing. She smirks. "Well damn, Lei, I don't think I've ever seen anybody bliss out over bread and jam before," she says as her smirk continues to grow. "Guess you don't even need me anymore."

I swallow my food quickly and summon up my royal dignity. "You know well by now that your surface commonalities are mostly new experiences for me," I say lightly, determined not to let her fluster me. "I'll not be made to feel embarrassed simply by my sampling new things."

Captain Vine only grins and turns to Amarante. "D'you make that yourself?" she asks, nodding at the goop jar.

"I do, actually," the healer answers, looking with an amused smile between us. "Several kinds of berry grow wild just beyond the tree line."

"Hmm. We'll hafta check that out while we're here," my Captain decides, cutting into her own white and yellow puddles. "And now I think Lorelei may wanna bring you with us when we leave to make her breakfast every morning." She winks at me as she finally takes her first bite of food.

I turn away from both of them with my brown sponge and purple goo — my bread and jam, as it is apparently called. I am not sure which substance is the bread and which is the jam, but there is no way that I'm asking that question while that smirk is still sitting on my Captain's face.

"Actually …" I hear Captain Vine say thoughtfully after a moment. "Hey, Amarante. You busy much the rest of the day?"

Curious, I risk giving them my attention again. The healer seems just as curious as I. "I've no prior appointments, if that's what you mean," she says. "I had planned to repair my front window and perhaps gather some herbs afterward if time permitted. Why, what do you need?"

"I have an idea," is all my Captain answers with. "I'm not sure if it'll work, but I think you might find it interesting. Can you come with us to my ship after breakfast?"

***

The white and yellow puddle things are apparently some sort of egg, although they look and taste nothing like any eggs I have ever eaten before, and I wonder what manner of fish may have laid them. They remind me somewhat of oysters, slimy and vaguely meaty. I still prefer the bread and jam, though.

After this final breakfast lesson, and after the meal itself, the three of us return to the deck of *The Queen's Runner*. Though we collect a few suspicious looks from the men and women working the modest docks, I soon realize that they are directed not at us but at Amarante. My Captain and I, to all appearances, are simply two more normal travelers. The distrustfulness raised in the villagers by Amarante's magic, however, apparently follows her around even when she is not actively practicing it.

Though it is not intended for me, it still makes me uneasy to pass through their gazes. The mob in Rockquay had much the same look about them once my Captain's true nature was discovered. Amarante, for her part, either does not appear to notice or else has perfected the appearance of not appearing to notice.

"Not to seem rude, Captain Vine," the healer says as we cross the deck of my Captain's ship, "but is there a need to continue withholding the details of your request from me?"

My Captain stops with her hand on the door of the cabin, glancing out over the railing at the people milling about on the pier. Apparently satisfied that nobody can overhear her, she turns to Amarante. "I'd like you to try and fix my ship, please."

Amarante's brows scrunch in confusion. "I'm sorry if I gave the wrong impression, Captain, but I don't think I'm qualified," she answers. "I can board up a broken window competently enough now, but that's about the extent of my carpentry skills, I'm afraid."

My Captain grins and opens the door. "I'm not asking for a carpenter," she says, gesturing us inside. "I'd like you to use your spirit magic on it."

Amarante turns her confused expression on me. I can only offer a shrug. I do not know where this is going either. "I … don't think my particular talents will work on something like a ship, Captain Vine," she explains.

Vine only turns and leads us into the cabin. "They might work on mine," she says.

Confused but intrigued, the two of us follow her down the short and narrow hallway of the small cabin, past the only bedroom, the storage closet, and the small kitchen area. At the end of the hallway is a ladder disappearing down a latch to whatever waits below the deck. I reflect that for all of my days spent on this ship already, I have never once been below deck, though Captain Vine inevitably makes at least one trip down every day. She has not exactly forbidden me from following her, but neither has she offered to show me where she goes. I, for my part, have never given it a good deal of thought until now.

She puts a foot on the ladder and takes a step down through the opening, then turns and looks earnestly at Amarante. "I'm about to put a good deal of trust in you, Amarante," she says, her tone completely serious. "I do this because I've done so already and you've shown that you can be depended upon with it so far. I do, however, both ask and insist that you not speak of what you're about to see to anyone else unduly. Is this alright?"

Amarante frowns and takes a hesitant step backward. "Captain Vine, if I may be blunt, you're beginning to worry me," the healer confides. "Just what are you asking me to do here? What do you have that is so secretive that it warrants this behavior?"

"Nothing so heinous as you may be thinking, I assure you," says my Captain. "But, between my race and your talents, we both know what it's like to have things that are better left unaired whenever possible." She smiles then, an attempt to lighten the mood. "This is one of those things. A fairy thing. Spreading word about it won't hurt anybody but me."

Amarante frowns thoughtfully and says nothing for several moments, considering. Soon, though, she nods her head. "I suppose I can understand," she says, stepping toward the ladder again. "But I still cannot promise anything."

"Fair enough," says my Captain, then disappears down the ladder. We follow suit, though I am once again the least graceful of the three of us as I work out how to climb down without dropping myself. My only experience with ladders so far has been the short one leading up the wall of the cabin to the upper portion of the deck where the ship's wheel sits. This one is longer, the space tighter and dark, the terrain below unknown. Still, I believe I do fairly well.

The space below the deck is even taller than the cabin, though more cluttered. Light filters in sparingly through the thin spaces between deck boards further into the room, beyond the bounds of the cabin above us. Wooden containers in a myriad of shapes sit stacked and clustered around in the gloom. Most of them are open and empty, presumably a result of the seizure of the ship's goods by the Rockquay authority. We pick our way through the cluster of containers toward the center of the space. As we go, the floor beneath our feet becomes lumpier, less even. I look down and see what looks like a bed of thick roots threading along the floor — and through it. I realize then that there are no boards on the floor or walls in here. Somehow, the inside of the below deck area is one solid, root-filled piece of wood.

As it happens, I do not have long to wonder about this. Captain Vine leads us to the center of the area, where all containers have been cleared away. Here, sprouting straight up from the floor of the deck, is the source of the oddity. Even with my limited knowledge of what counts for normal up here above the water, I know enough to realize how strange this is.

Amarante realizes it too, as her eyes widen visibly in the sparse light as we approach it. "How is …?" she starts, then turns to my Captain. "There is a tree growing out of your ship!"

"Actually," says Captain Vine, "it would be more accurate to say there's a ship growing out of my tree."

There is indeed a tree, though smaller than those uncountable numbers towering over the edge of Waterglade. The thick wooden roots on the floor all converge in a tangled mass at the center of the room, then form into a single solid shoot only about as thick as one of my thighs. This juts upward, crooked in intervals, almost touching the roof of the deck above us, with similar growths on a smaller scale reaching out from it toward the thin cracks above and the slight sunlight filtering through them. Peppered throughout the whole of the thing are flat, wide blades of dark green vegetation, similar in shape to an open hand and about half as big as one of my own.

I admit, I find this a strange addition to the rest of the ship. Captain Vine, for her part, is obviously unaffected by the sight, familiar as it must be to her. Amarante, however, gives it the same look of awe that she had given me upon learning that I were a mermaid.

"How is this even possible?" she asks my Captain after several stunned moments.

Captain Vine's lips draw together in a pensive line. "It's a long story," she replies. "The short answer is that it's a fae ship."

"I was not even aware that the fae built seafaring ships," Amarante replies, stepping closer toward the growth. She reaches out to run a hand gently along the surface of its main shoot, as if testing to see if it is real.

"They … don't have that many of them," my Captain says, looking from the tree to the healer. "This one has a lot of additions in the human style. Very little of the deck is live growth, and the cabin is only a basic framework with walls built onto it afterward. But for the most part, the shape and body of the ship stem from this one." She steps forward then as well, brushing her fingers lovingly along the nearest and smallest offshoot of the main body, lightly caressing the green vegetation on the end as if it were one of the most delicate things in the world.

"Incredible," Amarante breathes, stepping back again.

"Yes," says my Captain. "But wilting." She looks at the healer then, an urgency in her expression. "I'd like you to revitalize it if at all possible, please. It's grown weaker of late, and the integrity of the ship as a whole is suffering for it. The additional construction is loosening as it weakens, and the first stages of rot are beginning to set in to the hull, I can feel it."

"I ... have never performed my magic on a tree before, even a normal one," the healer admits hesitantly. "In theory it should work. It is as much a living thing as the rest of us, I suppose. But the life in question will be a foreign one to my control." She looks at my Captain then, mouth set in a firm line, eyes full of purpose. "I can make no promises, but I will try my best," she says.

Captain Vine smiles, then suddenly steps forward and wraps her arms around the shorter young woman, drawing her into a snug embrace. As we are of similar size, Amarante's face presses to the same place in my Captain's cleavage that mine usually does. From what little I can see of her face around my Captain's bust, the healer looks surprised but not discomfited by the action.

"Thank you," Captain Vine says, the tone of her voice reflecting her spoken gratitude. "You don't know how big a favor this is you're doing me." She steps back then, releasing Amarante, the curved wooden charm around her neck bouncing lightly out of its usual resting spot between her breasts after being dislodged by the force of the hug. "Oh," my Captain says as an afterthought, lifting the charm between them. She reaches behind her neck then and unfastens the necklace, handing it out toward Amarante. "This might help. It's magically connected to *The Queen's Runner*."

"What is it?" the healer asks, taking it gently and turning it over in her fingers.

"It's the heartwood of the parent growth," my Captain explains. "It helps me guide the ship." She reaches out then to take Amarante's hands in her own, closing both of their fingers over the talisman. "It is also one of the most precious things that I own. Please be careful with it."

"Of course, Captain," says Amarante. They step away from one another then, the healer turning back to the small tree. "I'll begin at once. But I may need to get a feel for the energy involved here before I can start the repair in earnest. It may be some time before I am finished."

"That's fine," says Captain Vine, walking over to me and draping an arm over my shoulders. "We've got some errands to run in town, and I think we'll be heading into the forest afterward. We'll be back here before nightfall."

"Would you mind collecting a few things for me while you're in the forest?" Amarante asks.

A few minutes later, my Captain and I are stepping off the deck of *The Queen's Runner* by ourselves, both of us with directions around town and a list of plants to look out for floating through our minds courtesy of Amarante. "If we're a little bit luckier and we stretch our money tight," says my Captain to me, "we might actually get out of here with most of what we need after all."

I nod, then turn around to look back at the ship floating in the harbor.

Captain Vine notices and quirks an eyebrow. "What's up?" she asks.

"*The Queen's Runner* really *is* a vegetable," I answer, looking at it in a new light. "I was right after all."

My Captain's brow scrunches up for a moment, then she sighs and shakes her head. "Yes, Lorelei," she says, patting me on top of my head. "If you look at it that way, I suppose it is. C'mon, we got shopping to do."

***

The rest of our day speeds by in a blur of business, the both of us trekking across the town and back again, readying our ship and ourselves for our eventual departure.

First, after leaving Amarante in the hold of *The Queen's Runner,* Captain Vine and I locate the local clothier. Here we allow ourselves enough leeway with our money for both of us to purchase a fresh new outfit, bringing our total up to two each. My Captain selects an off-white shirt that she calls a blouse, with ruffles along the edges and a simple round fastener in the front that she calls a button. Like her previous outfit, it hides very little of her; the low neckline drapes off of her shoulders and leaves her arms bare, and the plunge in the front and abrupt end on the bottom leave her abdomen and ample cleavage freely exposed.

She is proud of her cleavage, I have come to notice. For my part, I cannot say that I blame her.

Complimenting this top is a pair of pants much like those that she had already, except a light shade of brown that matches the wood of her ship. These sit low on her hips and hug her curves below them tightly all the way down to just below her knees, where they abruptly end and her boots begin.

For myself, I choose another simple dress like the one I have been wearing already. I have no desire to try and maneuver my legs into a pair of pants, especially a pair as snug as my Captain has chosen. Instead I choose a white dress of soft, loose fabric that gathers beneath my breasts and drapes comfortably down to my mid-thigh. The top and bottom are both ruffled like my Captain's blouse, and thin, diaphanous straps going over my shoulders hold the whole ensemble up.

In addition, I get a new hat, also white and with a very wide brim, accented with a trailing blue ribbon. I had had one much like it in Rockquay before losing it in the water during our escape, and I partially blame its absence for the extent of my sunburn. As pleasant as the treatment for it may have been, I've no desire to relive that particular injury again if at all possible.

After clothes shopping, I expect us to head straight into the nearby forest, excited as my Captain has been by the sight of it ever since we landed. First, however, she wishes to see to our other supply needs. "There are things we won't be able to find in the woods," she explains. "The sooner we get those out of the way, the less of a hurry we have to be in to get our forest trip done and over with."

So instead, we pay visits to several of the fishermen and boat wrights around the dock, whom my Captain asks about procuring these supplies. They point her to several buildings scattered across the water's edge, and after paying each a visit for discussion and haggling, we are back on the deck of *The Queen's Runner,* my Captain directing the handful of men walking to and fro across the ship. Each comes aboard carrying a new bundle of supplies: dense coils of thick rope, folded bolts of sturdy cloth, stacked piles of cut wooden boards, sealed barrels of unknown content, and more necessities of a healthy ship that are not immediately apparent until they are found lacking. Captain Vine has some of these stored in the supply closet, some on the deck by the cabin door, some in the small galley, and some in the only bedroom. She lets nobody into the hold, however, where Amarante and the strange tree are hidden away together.

The sun has passed by overhead and begun its descent toward the horizon when a young boy scurries up to the edge of the pier and stands watching the men at their labor. My Captain catches his eye and smiles at him, at which point he blushes and fidgets with the hem of his coarse and oversized shirt. Half an hour later and he is still standing there, still watching the activity and casting the occasional furtive glance at my Captain. At last, she crosses to the edge of the deck, leaning over the railing and smiling at the boy. "Something I can help you with, young sir?" she asks.

The boy blushes again but nods frantically, reaching into his pocket and pulling out a scrap of parchment, which he holds out to my Captain. She, for her part, flashes me a look of confusion before bounding over the railing to the deck near the boy. "You're the captain here, ma'am?" he asks, looking up at her.

"I am," I hear her reply.

He holds the parchment up to her again. "A man gave me a silver piece and told me to give this to the lady captain of a ship called *The Queen's Runner* if it ever showed up," he explains.

Captain Vine's brow only furrows deeper, but she takes the parchment from the boy and hands him a copper piece for his troubles with her thanks. With another graceful jump, she boards the ship again as the young man scurries away. She turns her confusion on me yet again, then on the paper. "Wonder who knew I'd be coming by here," she says aloud, unfolding the letter.

At that moment, however, Amarante appears above deck and calls to us, her breath coming hard and fast. We turn at her approach and notice the remaining dock workers scowl and back away out of her path as she walks over to us. Again, if she notices their open aversion of her, she gives no indication.

"What's up?" my Captain asks, absently tucking the letter into her pocket, momentarily forgotten.

The healer takes a deep breath and wipes a light sweat from her brow. "I am afraid … I can do no more today …" she says breathily, her chest heaving slowly. "We are progressing better than I thought, but … the work is still slow. Touch and go. I will need to finish up tomorrow."

Captain Vine grins widely and pulls Amarante into a sudden hug, squishing her new top against the healer's face. "You're awesome, Amy," she says before releasing her. Amarante's cheeks look flushed as she pulls away, though I cannot tell if it is embarrassment or exertion that stains them.

"I was thinking of heading home for dinner now," says the healer. "You two are welcome to join me, of course."

We take her up on her offer and return to her combination house and healing clinic.

Dinner, as it turns out, is a pot of mixed vegetables and some chunks of meat of unknown origin to me, all boiled together in water thick with their varied flavors. Another new culinary experience for me, but one more easily tackled than breakfast had been. Captain Vine scoops the meat from her own bowl into mine, waving away Amarante's concerns over the food and explaining that she simply prefers not to eat any meat.

I have no such qualms. After adding a generous amount of salt to the meal, it even tastes somewhat familiar, reminding me of the food back home. I feel a pang of homesickness then, but smaller than what I am used to. I suppose I am enjoying myself too much of late to be overly nostalgic.

My Captain and I offer to help Amarante around her shop after dinner as our way of saying thank you yet again for all of her hospitality. She accepts, and while she and I organize the contents of her medicinal shelf in the front of her shop, Captain Vine carries things to and from the storage area at the healer's behest.

I am watching Amarante crush some sort of dried berry into a small glass jar, ready to shelve it once she has finished, when my Captain returns with a quizzical look on her face and something in her hand. "Amy?" she asks, holding the item up for inspection, "What is this?"

It's a good question, for I have no idea what it is she holds either. It looks like a slightly curved tube, about a foot long from tip to tip, coated in some sort of pink, semi-transparent substance much like the jam from breakfast, only solidified. Both ends of the thing sport a round, knobbed head, while the middle is bisected by a pad of what looks like leather, with several straps hanging off of it.

Amarante looks up at the object and shrugs. "It's a device I use for my healing," she says simply.

Captain Vine is still staring at the object in confusion and, it seems, a bit of amusement, for some reason. "How?" she asks.

"It's a crystal core wrapped in a soft protective resin," the healer explains. "You remember how I told you that the more serious the injury or illness is in a patient, the deeper I have to reach into them with my magic?" She nods to the object in my Captain's hands. "The crystal encased in that device is conductive to magical energy. It allows me to reach a deeper connection with my patients than I otherwise could on my own."

My Captain turns the thing over and over in her hands, amusement growing as the healer's explanation dispels her confusion. "You know what it looks like, right?" she asks.

Amarante nods. "How do you think it's used?"

My Captain stops her inspection of the thing and looks up suddenly at the healer. "What?"

Amarante smiles patiently. “I know what you’re thinking, Captain Vine. And you’re right. It’s used pretty much in the same way that I can tell you’re imagining right now.” She glances sidelong at me, then, for some reason. “Crystal conductors are not uncommon among magical practitioners where I was taught. The design on this one is meant to make deep spirit magic between two women easier to perform.”

My Captain actually giggles through her grin. Amarante is still smiling politely. For myself, I get the feeling that some part of this discussion has passed over my head. “Honestly,” says Captain Vine, “I would not have thought to find something like this in your shop, Amy.”

“And why not?” asks the healer.

“Well,” says my Captain, “from the way you hesitated and blushed when fixing my burns meant giving me a kiss, I thought you’d be as embarrassingly prude as the rest of the humans I’ve been meeting in my travels.”

“I’m a mage and a healer, Captain,” says Amarante, sounding slightly offended. “Magic requires what it requires, and I see no reason to approach the body or its uses with undue squeamishness. Touching their vital essence is about as intimate as you can get with another person. Once you can do that, why stay reserved about the lesser considerations?”

“Can I borrow it?” my Captain asks, eyes suddenly on me with that hungry look in them that I’ve come to know so well. I’ve no idea why she would need it for what her gaze tells me she now has in mind, but I feel my own body responding to her look in that now-familiar way. It *has* been several days since the last time we did that together, I think to myself. I am not sure what surprises me more about the thought — that my

Captain could keep her hands off of me for so long, or that I apparently am just as eager for her to put them back on me as she is.

Amarante looks between us, and the intent there must be so obvious as to be made visible. "I, uh … I'd actually prefer if you didn't," she says, her gaze apologetic on both of us. "It's not really a toy, you see. And it's one of the most valuable things that I own."

"Oh." My Captain's expression drops instantly into a pronounced pout, like a scolded child. "Alright then," she says, the picture of dejection. "I'll go put it back."

"Sorry," says the healer as my Captain leaves the room.

Strangely, I feel sorry as well, though for what I do not know.

***

Naturally, after the look we shared in Amarante's front room over the strange device, my Captain and I enter our room together that night already knowing what it is we are about to do.

No words have passed between us since bidding the healer goodnight, but I can see by the glimmer in her eye when she looks at me what she is thinking. I blush accordingly, though by now I believe it is probably more of a habitual response than anything. Truth be told, I am at least as eager as she by now.

No sooner do I close the door of the small bedroom we have been granted and turn toward Captain Vine then she is on me, her mouth cutting off both the small talk that I had first planned and the sound of surprise that has sprung suddenly to my lips. Warm and soft, her lips enwrap my own as she presses me tight to the closed door with her presence. I feel the heat and passion emanating off of her and flowing over me like the tide, yet never receding, only advancing.

It is a familiar feeling, yet stronger than I am used to, and it pushes all of the heat within me instantly to the surface, making my head swim. It is much, I realize, like the intense and confusing passion of our very first meeting aboard her ship, back when I had every reason to run yet did not, and not entirely because I was chained up at the time.

When my Captain pulls her mouth from mine finally, I gasp in a faltering breath that turns into something between a moan and a whimper, and my eyes have difficulty focusing on her as I find myself sliding bodily down the door to the floor. "Whoa," my Captain breathes, a look of pleasant surprise on her own face. "So, that's back on. And from the look of you down there, it's even stronger than usual. Must be the magic exposure."

"What …?" is all that I can gasp out at the moment as I look up at her. Though my head feels light and my vision unfocused, she stands out clear and beautiful in my sight, smiling mischievously down at me. When she leans over toward me, I feel another wash of that strange passion coming off of her, as if the very air around her is caressing me lovingly.

"You remember I told you about the fae aura?" she asks me, kneeling down to my level. "How we bewitch those around us with an innate magic that we can never quite turn off? And how mine was partially to blame for charming you to me?"

I nod, faintly recalling the conversation through the more pressing direction in which my thoughts are turning.

"Yeah," she says, then leans in closer and kisses me again, sending a hot chill trembling through the whole of my body. "It's back now," she whispers with a smile against my lips. "With a vengeance. Thank Amarante's healing." Then she presses herself to me a third time, and more than just her mouth.

I am not sure when she stops again, if it has been several minutes or a mere moment. "C-can you … control it n-now?" I manage to pant out as my breathing quickens yet further.

"I think I could," she replies, "if I tried. I'm not going to." Then her hands are in my hair, her fingers brushing through the red strands, and her shirt is gone somewhere. Bare, creamy, light brown skin fills my vision as she pulls me toward her, and my lips land against her body in a hungry kiss.

She is warm, and soft, and beneath my mouth, she is delicious. I kiss her again and again, not caring where, not bothering to see what part of her my lips are caressing as she holds me to her. From the sound of her breathing and the way her chest swells beneath me, I do not think that she cares where I aim my affection either.

I almost protest when she pushes me away some time later, but then her hands are beneath my dress, lifting it, and now my own body is bared before her, and it is her turn to taste me. My head rolls back as she deftly captures one of my breasts in her mouth, her hands on my naked back holding me close to her as she kisses and licks the aching bud of my nipple. We are both still on the hard wooden floor of the bedroom, and yet I feel as if I am floating in the warmest and gentlest of waters, being lapped at by strange and exciting currents.

She trails her lips all across the front of me, from my neck down to my navel and back, and all I can do is gasp and moan and dig my fingers into the warm skin of her strong, bare back. My chest and hips roll independently of my thoughts beneath her, the former with breath that becomes harder and harder to manage, the latter with a surging, liquid need for more. Then she stands, pulling me up with her, first to my knees, then to shaky and uncertain legs. "Captain ..." I breathe, and her hands are on me as she leads me to the bed, stroking fire out of my flesh until I feel I shall burn up from the inside out.

"Lay down, Lorelei," she whispers into my ear, and I do as she bids, lying back on the bed and reaching up to her, trying to bring her down with me and entangle myself in her once more.

She takes my hand and kisses it gently, then smiles and steps back from the bed. "Oh, hush," she chides as I whimper slightly in protest. "You've lasted this long without melting. You'll probably last another few seconds." She grins at me, then slowly, achingly slowly, lifts each leg in turn and slips her boots off of her calves to the floor. I swallow hard and watch from my position sprawled across our bed as she hooks her thumbs into the hem of her pants and gently wiggles them down her hips, then her legs, her perfect, gorgeous legs. They slip free to puddle around her feet, and with a light kick she sends them backwards through the air, where they land on her shirt and my dress on the other side of the room.

"Oh Captain …!" I breathe, reaching for her again as she slinks slowly back toward the bed. She takes my hand and props one of her knees up on the mattress, then puts my fingers to the inside of her thigh. I bite my lip as she slides my hand gently up her soft brown skin, feeling the graceful muscles beneath, and then my hand is cupping the slit between her thighs, already as warm and moist as I feel all over myself. I gently slide my fingers along the heat of the lips here, moaning as I do so as if it is myself that I am caressing. Captain Vine groans deep in her throat, her eyes slipping closed. Her hand not holding mine slides up her body to cup her own ample breast, kneading the soft mound as her hips rock slowly against my touch. And all the while I feel her heat pulsing through the air, wafting over me and through me as her own passion turns outward through the strange power of her fae aura.

Within seconds, it is clear that she is losing her calm control of the situation as well. Her eyes slip shut, her wet lips part and seem to try and pull my finger inside. I oblige and slip it between the hot folds of her dripping softness, and am rewarded for my actions by watching my Captain's mouth part in an audible gasp as her body shudders with excitement.

It is too much, seeing this pleasure run through her, feeling it wash out onto my own body. I moan deep, my head falling back against the bed, my eyes slipping shut as I surrender myself totally to the heat of the moment. Then my Captain's fingers are caressing me as well between my trembling thighs, and in the suddenness of the contact I cannot stifle the gasp of surprise that forces its way out of me.

The next several minutes, or hours, or however long they last, are unbearable. Her fingers on me, mine in her, both of us squirming against one another's touch, melting inside and dripping out over each other's hands. With my eyes half lidded, I can barely make out the glorious image of her grinding her hips into my outstretched palm, her face the picture of hungry ecstasy that I feel on myself as well. The air is full of our combined passion, of our comingled moans and gasps and labored breathing, growing stronger and louder by the moment, all of it wrapped in the heat of her aura, surrounding us, enveloping us, coaxing us further and further still, stoking the flames hotter and hotter —

I cry out suddenly, a strained and high-pitched noise that cuts off barely out of my lips, as I feel the heat inside me break and crash down around me, on me, sweeping me up and carrying me away as my body throbs uncontrollably in that way that I have come to know and now relish. My full focus, or what is left of it, is upon my Captain's finger curled up inside me as I wrap myself around it and hold on for dear life. Despite all of this, my own hand is still somehow cupped around her hot, wet softness, one finger slipped deep inside of her and still moving, as if trying to pull her down into my own helpless ecstasy.

It works. As I begin the slow drift down from the crescendo of my lust, I feel the weight of the bed shift. When I can focus my vision enough to look up, I see Captain Vine bent low over me, her hair brushing my face, her own face only inches from mine. Up close, her labored breathing washes warm against my skin, her quick, frantic moaning drowning out my own panting. Her eyes, unfocused, look down into my own as if searching for me, and by the gods, at that moment, she looks so desperate and helpless that I almost do not recognize her.

"Lei," she gasps, her chest heaving against mine, her wetness throbbing and trembling in my hand, "Lei, I, I'm —!" Her attempt at speech catches in a long, drawn-out whimper, and she bites her lip against it as I feel her entire self tremble and release, as I push her past the breaking point of her own passion. It shatters and flows out over my fingers, slick and juicy, and I feel the shock of it through her throbbing aura of fae magic as if I am experiencing it myself all over again. She collapses onto me then, her cheek pressed tight to mine, one of her hands gripping the sheet by my head as if to let go of it would mean to float away. Her other hand is still firmly cupped around my own slick wetness, her finger still buried in me, as her own throbs hard and squeezes frantically with her crescendoing lust. I wrap my other arm around her, holding her tight to me and burying my fingers in the waves of her hair, and together we wash away in the wake of our combined pleasure.

It is a long time before either of us comes down enough to think of the world outside our own bodies once again. My Captain is the first to get her voice back, and she laughs, low and weak, into the curve where my neck meets my shoulder. "I, uh … I had planned for more than just that …" she says, her voice muffled. "I was going to do so much more to you … I had ideas …"

“It was enough,” I breathe, smiling. We still have our hands between each other’s legs, and I gently and idly run my finger back and forth over her lips there.

“Mmm … For now,” she murmurs, rising up on one arm and gazing down at me. In her eyes is that strange look she often has for me that I have come to know. A kind of possessive tenderness. Despite the friendliness of our interactions, in her mind, I know, I belong to her as surely as her ship.

I do not mind.

We sleep where we lie that night, neither of us bothering to rise after our activities together in bed. Captain Vine gets her fae aura under control again, I assume, for the heady urgency that it had been affecting in me departs, leaving the both of us awash in deep contentment as we drift off in each other’s arms, too tired and entangled in one another to know which limb belongs to whom and too happy to care.

I do not realize in the moment that this is the last time I will see my Captain so carefree for a long while.

***

The next morning has only barely begun to dawn when I awaken, sprawled out alone on the bed. The first dim rays of sun are barely peeking through the room’s only window, the stars still out in the lightening blue sky. With this scant illumination I can make out Captain Vine sitting on the foot of the bed, fully clothed down to the sword hanging from her hip. Her hands sit in her lap, clenched tight around a scrap of paper, and she is rocking slightly, back and forth, on the bed.

I stir only barely when her head snaps around to pin me with her gaze. “You’re awake,” she says brusquely, and rises from the bed, striding across the room quick enough to almost be called running. “Here,” she says, snatching my dress from the floor and tossing it to me on the bed. “Get dressed. We have to go.”

“Go?” I ask, rubbing the sand of sleep from my eyes and trying to catch up with my still-drowsy mind.

“Leave,” she says, striding back to the bed, then up and down the length of it seemingly for lack of any other action to take. “We have to get out of Waterglade and back to sea. We’ve spent long enough in this town.”

“We’ve spent … two nights and a day,” I say, memory coming slowly this soon after wakening. “That is not so terribly long.”

“It’s long enough,” my Captain insists. “We got what we needed.”

“We have not yet journeyed into the nearby forest,” I point out. “You wanted to gather some things from there, yes? Perhaps we can go today and —”

“No!” she snaps, freezing in her pacing. Her hands clench so tightly around the paper in them that I can hear it rip. “No,” she says more calmly, but just barely. “We took too long. There’s no time left. Maybe … maybe next time.”

I furrow my brow in confusion, but she is not looking at me, just staring at a point in the middle distance with a look nearing panic. “But you were so looking forward to it,” I protest quietly. “You spoke of trees. You sounded so excited.”

She makes no move and says nothing, just takes a long, deep breath and exhales shakily. "Put your dress on, Lorelei," she commands after a moment. "I'm going to go settle things with Amarante. Then we sail."

She turns on her heel, then, and rushes from the room with no further explanation, leaving me to my dressing and my profound concern.

***

By the time I am clothed and heading downstairs, the sun has risen no higher. From the flicker of firelight coming from the main room, I see that Amarante is up herself, and I hear her talking with my Captain as I walk in. She sounds almost as confused as I from what I catch of their conversation.

"… seaworthy enough, perhaps," the healer is saying. "But your, uh … tree-ship is still half wilted. I'd planned to finish tending to it later today."

"What would happen if we sailed out on it right now?" my Captain asks, still no calmer judging by the tone of her voice.

"I cannot be certain," Amarante replies. "All I know of ships, I know secondhand simply from my time living in this town. But I imagine you could get a short ways down the coast before you faced the same problems you had when you first docked."

Captain Vine brings her thumb up to her mouth and bites down on the nail, staring urgently at nothing for a silent moment. "Not to the next town, you think?"

"Perhaps," says the healer, "but in truth, the bulk of the work is still to be done today. Yesterday was mostly my determining how to apply my methods to a tree that is also a ship, somehow. And, if I may be frank, I am still offering to make the repairs for free. I doubt you'll find a shipwright here or in the next town making the same offer, and I know you'll find no more spirit mages anywhere in the southern United Freelands."

"Mab's tits," I hear my Captain mumble under her breath, and she glances searchingly around the dimly lit room. Her eyes pass over me as if I am simply one more object to take into her consideration, and then she looks back to the healer. "Can you start now?" she asks.

"I … suppose, yes," says Amarante, and it sounds as if she is growing flustered with this strange urgency of Captain Vine's. "My herb stocks are not yet organized to my liking, and I really must see to the window." She indicates with a look the broken glass of the front window, still open to the dawn breeze. "If I do not board it up soon, I'll only be asking for thievery. I had planned on seeing to that first today, but —"

"We'll take care of it," my Captain says, cutting her off. "Me and Lorelei. We'll fix your shop up for you while you work on the *Runner*."

Amarante casts a questioning look at me, but all I can do is return it with a nod. I know nothing of my Captain's mood either, but if this is what she desires, I am not averse to lending my aid to her plan.

"I suppose that will work," the healer replies. "Would you like breakfast first, or —?"

"No," my Captain interrupts. "Thank you. The sooner this is done, the better."

"Captain Vine." Amarante sets her portable fire device down on her counter and looks earnestly at my Captain. "It takes no insight to notice that something is troubling you. Are you able to share with me what it is?"

"I …" For a moment, my Captain glances between the healer and me, and the worry is so profound on her face that I fear I start to catch it myself, though I know not why. "… No," she says at last. "No, I … I'd better not. Call it another esoteric fae thing."

"The fae are not so esoteric as you might think to those of us unafraid enough to learn what we can of them," Amarante answers with a thoughtful frown. "But, if you insist, then I will trust your judgment. Let me gather a few things and I will make my way to your ship."

"Thank you," my Captain breathes as if in relief. "You've no idea what a help that is to me."

"No, I fear I do not," says the healer as she passes me by. We share the same confused look, and then she turns back to Captain Vine in the doorway. "And I see I am not the only one, Captain Vine," she adds, glancing pointedly at me. "Whatever eats at you, were I you, I would consider sharing it with those I trust."

"I …" My Captain lifts her other hand and glances down at it. The scrap of paper from earlier is still crushed within her tight grip, and she regards it with a strange intensity. "Perhaps," she says after a moment. "In time." And then, slowly but far from calm, she shreds the paper into tiny scraps.

Amarante says nothing, only disappears through the doorway to go collect her things.

***

The rest of our morning is awkward, to say the least. My Captain has me assist her in hauling several of the wooden boards from up Amarante's stairs down into the front room, though we do not speak as we do so, and still do not afterward. Instead, Captain Vine disappears again into the rear of the building, leaving me to pick up where Amarante and I had left off the previous night with organizing her herb collection.

This I do for all of several seconds before my eyes fall on the empty stone alcove against one of the room's side walls. This Amarante had called her fireplace, a special standing pit in which to safely build a fire without it consuming the wood of the rest of the building. It is empty now but for some black, brittle pieces of wood and what looks like a pile of soft gray sand — and the shredded scraps of the paper to which my Captain had been clinging all morning.

I cast a quick glance at the doorway to make sure that Captain Vine is not returning yet, then quickly set my task down and cross to the fireplace, in front of which I kneel. The paper scraps are lying on the mound of gray sand, which is strangely fluffy to the touch; and as I scoop them up, much of the powdered wood sand comes with me on the skin of my hands. I brush this off as best I can and arrange the paper on the floor in front of the fireplace, trying to piece it back together. The powdery sand stuff clings to this too, however, obscuring most of the words. Between that and the shredding my Captain had inflicted on it, I can only barely make out some of what it says:

You know…annot run foreve…
…will find…drag you h…

It is the letter handed to my Captain by the young boy on the dock yesterday, I realize. The one that she had been distracted from reading. Now she had read it, and whatever message it held, it was to blame for her sudden and intense change of both plan and mood.

"Lorelei!" she calls from the room beyond, and I jump clumsily to my feet with a start. "I need you to come here!"

"A moment, please!" I call back, brushing the scraps back into the fireplace with my feet. My hands are still stained with the evidence of what I had been doing when I join my Captain in the small storage area of Amarante's building, but I do not think she notices. Faraway as her thoughts are, I do not think she would notice even had I arrived naked, sprouting wings like a gull.

"I need you to help with these nails, please," she says with a gesture to a nearby glass jar and without looking at me. "I can't touch them. Didn't think about that when I volunteered for this task."

Dutifully I grab the jar, glancing inside at the tiny iron spikes jumbled together like a metal urchin. "Captain —" I say, but when I turn to her I find she is already gone, striding back to the front room. With a sigh, I follow.

Together, we repair Amarante's window from the inside of her shop. My Captain and I lift the boards in place together, then I hold the little iron spikes, called nails, in their correct place while Captain Vine pounds them into the wood with another lump of solid iron on the end of a wooden stick. This, too, seems uncomfortable for her, but she only grimaces and continues in silent concentration, staring equally at the task at hand and her own inner thoughts. I do not try again to breach the topic hanging over us, only aid her in this task in silence and wonder how best to aid her in her mood.

We are about to lift the last board into place when we see, in the gap above our handiwork, the mob coming toward us on the streets outside, the brightening morning sun and the light of the fires they carry glinting off of the many bared metal implements in their hands.

"By all the — you've gotta be fucking kidding me!" my Captain all but screams. "Lorelei, get down!" Without waiting to see if I comply, she grabs me about the shoulders and shoves us both to the floor, kneeling beneath the boarded up window flat against the wall.

From this position, we hear the steady grumbling of the crowd grow louder as it grows closer. A moment later, a man's voice is shouting in our direction. "Come out of there, you elf-loving witch! You knew this was coming!"

"Oh, by the Mother!" Captain Vine hisses to herself. "Can I go nowhere without being chased out of it anymore? How did they even find me out this time?"

"We know you're in league with that thrice-damned fae, witch!" the man's voice continues, and the crowd wordlessly adds its assent. "My boy says the bastard gave him a letter to deliver in secret to an accomplice of his! A letter that's ended up in *your* hands, you traitorous wench!" More shouting from the mob, growing louder and more outraged. “After all he did to harm this town, you have the gall to traffic with him?! We’ve stomached your magic ’til now, but this insult is too much, sorceress!”

“Wait, what?” my Captain asks, turning a quizzical look on me. “So it’s not me that’s set them off?”

For a moment, I am as surprised as she that she is not the target of their sudden malice. “It appears not,” I say. “Though considering our position, I’d not say that we’ve no concerns in this matter.”

“But if they don’t know about me yet,” Captain Vine thinks aloud, “then we’ve got a window. Lorelei,” she says, taking me by the shoulders and casting me a dire look, “grab a satchel and stuff it full of anything of Amarante’s that seems valuable or irreplaceable. As much of her belongings as you can carry.” She does not wait for me to comply before she herself scrambles from our spot beneath the boarded window and rushes from the room.

I follow her as far as the doorway. “Why are we taking Amarante’s things?” I call to her.

“Because I know how this is gonna play out!” she calls back amidst the sounds of frantic crashing and tinkling glass from the other room. “And we don’t have much time, so hurry!”

Between her tone and the growing noise of the angry mob outside, the immediacy of the situation becomes apparent, if not the explanation for it. Quickly I snatch up the first bag that I can find and begin piling the healer’s collection of stoppered jars and assorted little pouches into it, all of her medicinal stock that the two of us had been working on since yesterday. I know little about the potential value of anything else in her house, but luckily, at least for this exercise, she seems to have few personal effects around the place.

I am startled from my task by a sudden and violent pounding on the closed front door, and I am barely able to stifle a scream before it sounds again. Amarante, evidently, had locked the door behind her when she left. "You think to bar out the entire town, witch?" the man's voice calls through the wood, more menacing now that it is closer. "How many of us have you laid your hands on, eh? How many subjected themselves to your sorceries? How long did you think to lull our defenses by playing the concerned healer?" The pounding again, slower but heavier this time, and beneath that, I think I hear the wood begin to crack. "What other fae tricks have you learned, bitch?"

The mob sounds have also grown louder, closer, and through the gap of where the last board should have been nailed in over the window I can see faces approaching. I duck behind Amarante's counter before they see me, I hope, and eye the doorway to the next room, wondering if I dare try and slip through.

Then I hear something clatter to the floor from the other side of the counter and look up to see the light changed. The shadow of the counter is starker against the wall as flickering orange light plays across the room, like the light from Amarante's portable fire, but brighter. And slowly, to the sudden cheering of the mob outside, the air begins to change, growing warmer but with an acrid, unpleasant smell. I peek my head around the edge of the counter and risk a glance.

Beneath the window on which we had been working all morning, there is more fire than I have ever seen piled up at once, consuming the stick that it had been carried on and thrashing like a thing alive. And as I watch, it grows larger and begins to slowly climb the wall and crawl across the floor, grumbling and hissing in menace.

Caution bedamned, I rush from the room and into the next, stumbling in my haste. "Captain!" I call, not caring if those outside can hear me. "I think we have a problem!"

"Up here!" Captain Vine calls from the top of the stairs, and I run up after her, following her into the guest room that we've shared. I come in just in time to see her kick her entire boot through the only window, shattering the glass outward. She quickly kicks away the worst of the jagged shards remaining, then tosses the large and heavy looking canvas sack in her arms through the open portal. "You're not going to like this part," she says to me, then climbs onto the empty window ledge and, without a moment's thought, flings herself out of it.

I gasp and hurry to the window just in time to see her hit the ground rolling. She springs to her feet a second later, the skin of her arm cut shallowly and bleeding from the glass shards that she had just tumbled through, and looks frantically up at me.

"Throw me your satchel!" she says as loud as she dares. I unsling the pouch from my shoulder and toss it through the window into my Captain's waiting arms. She catches it deftly and drops it to the ground, her eyes still on me. "Good, now throw me you!"

"What?" I ask, hoping I've heard her amiss and eyeing the drop. She made it look easy, but we are two stories above the ground with only the empty air between I and it. I had never had a problem with heights or depths back home, but it suddenly occurred to me how much more menacing a couple dozen feet of vertical space could be here on land. "Captain, I don't think I can do what you just did!"

"I know!" she calls back. "I'll catch you, don't worry!"

I hesitantly half-climb onto the window's precipice, not any more at my ease for her assurance. "Will you really?" I ask.

"I'm fairly certain I will!" she calls back up. "I'll break your landing, if nothing else, and that's the best deal you're gonna get right now, Lei!"

Behind me, in the distance at the bottom of the stairs, I hear the sound of the front door crashing inward. Suddenly the air feels warmer on my back. "Gods below, what am I doing here?" I grumble to myself, then perch the rest of the way on the edge and leap.

True to her word, Captain Vine does her best to catch me. I end up crashing into her and sending us both sprawling to the ground, cutting our arms and legs anew on the shattered glass. It stings, and I believe we both gain our share of bruises from the attempt, but we have more pressing matters. A quick inspection reveals nothing broken on either of us and the cuts only shallow, and then my Captain is tugging me by the arm as we hurry from the healer's house and business through the shadows of the nearby buildings.

For good or for ill, we run into nobody else as we half sneak, half dash through the brightening town, sticking as close as we can to the smallest and most narrow of streets. For our sudden need to escape, this is a good sign, as it means less chance of having to repeat our time in Rockquay by fighting our way to freedom through innocent bystanders. But for Amarante's reputation and livelihood, this does not bode well, as it suggests that most of Waterglade has turned up to attack her home in a fit of anger.

We pause halfway through the town to catch our breath for a moment near the well where my Captain and I ate our first meal in days after first arriving here. I take the opportunity to look behind us, though I am not glad I did so. A black cloud is drifting quickly up in the distance from behind the buildings, near where Amarante's shop should be. Even here, we can hear the shouts of the crowd and the occasional violent crash. Whatever destruction is occurring, the villagers at least seem to be enjoying themselves.

Then Captain Vine grabs my arm and we continue our race toward *The Queen's Runner* before our otherness is discovered or somebody in the mob realizes that Amarante is not home to endure their wrath. We made no effort yesterday to hide our association with her or her presence on our ship. If we are not yet targets of Waterglade's ire, we soon will be.

All the while, I feel sick to my stomach. After everything that Amarante has done for us, all of the good that she has performed in this town, her reward is to lose her shop, her home, her livelihood, and, if this mob catches her and makes good on their anger, possibly her life.

Our first stroke of good luck, if indeed it can be called that, comes when we finally come in sight of the town docks. There amid the small fishing boats of the locals floats *The*

Queen's Runner, looking comparatively large and not apparently damaged.

"Thank the Mother," breathes Captain Vine. She doubles her speed, tugging me along the last stretch until we are pounding across the boards of the pier. My Captain quickly helps me onto the ship, then all but throws herself toward the door leading inside the cabin. I lean against the mast to catch my breath once more and gaze nervously at the rooftops nearby, waiting for the crowd to come rushing down the streets and attack us as well.

Before such a thing can happen, though, the winch beside the railing begins to turn of its own accord, hauling the anchor up from the water on its thick silver chain. I feel the ship lurch backward, sliding itself away from the docks, and hold on to the mast to steady myself, the sudden motion of sailing making me uneasy on my feet after our days on land.

The ship is still turning itself around when Captain Vine bursts through the door again with a whoop of joy, the sack of Amarante's belongings still slung over her shoulder and her familiar talisman dangling from one hand. "We're gonna make it, Lei!" she shouts as she clambers deftly up the ladder to the ship's wheel, which is also currently spinning itself. Her necklace she slips over her head to let the magic pendant settle back into its usual spot, then her hands are on the wheel and controlling it manually. I breathe a deep sigh of relief and watch as Waterglade spins away behind us.

We have only just begun moving forward out into open water when the door opens again and Amarante strides out wearing a concerned expression.

"Why are you two in such a —" she begins, then stops as she looks out over the front of the boat at the changed view. "Why are we — are we moving?" she demands, rushing to the side of the ship and looking over only to see Waterglade growing slowly smaller behind us. "Why are we moving?" she demands again, panicked, spinning around to cast a wide-eyed and accusatory glance at both me and Captain Vine above us. "Captain Vine, what are you doing? What's going on?"

"I'm saving us," Captain Vine answers shortly, not taking her eyes off of the horizon. "We're leaving Waterglade. Sorry for the short notice."

"Well, *I'm* not!" the healer shouts at her. "Turn around and take me back before you go sailing away on a whim! I'm sorry, I've tried to be accommodating, but this is further than I'm willing to go!"

"No, you're gonna wanna go a lot further before you stop, trust us," my Captain answers. "There's nothing for you back there. Nothing you'd care to be part of, anyway."

"I'll be the judge of that, Captain!" says the healer, settling her hands on her hips. She looks and sounds angrier than ever I have seen her so far. "I know it's not a perfect town, and I know what is thought of me, but my life is there, Captain Vine! My assignment! And I know you're no stranger to mistrust yourself, but that's not your —"

"Amarante," I say, and she turns her angry glare on me as I interrupt her. "I'm sorry," I continue, "truly. We both are. But my Captain is not exaggerating when she says that there is nothing for you back there. It's … it's gone."

Her anger visibly softens as her hands slip down from her hips. "What do you mean?" she asks quietly, though I can see realization dawning in her expression already.

I shake my head and cross the deck to her, wrapping her unbidden in a close embrace. "The townsfolk," I explain over her shoulder. "They formed a mob and stormed your shop. We barely escaped. It's …" I swallow a rising lump in my throat and hug her tighter. "You truly do not want to go back there, Amarante. There will be no home waiting for you, and no welcome, and no safety. It's all gone."

For a long moment she says and does nothing, only stands in my arms with her own hanging limp at her sides. I realize that, from where she stands, the black cloud rising up from her home should be visible in the distance behind the ship. If she will not believe us, perhaps catching sight of that will convince her.

Then, slowly, she lifts her hands and returns my embrace with a long, shuddering sigh. "You're telling the truth, aren't you?" she asks me quietly, though from her tone I can tell she already knows the answer. Her arms tighten around me, her body shaking slightly against my own. "I always knew it was a possibility, but still … to happen and be done with so suddenly …"

"I am sorry, Amarante," I whisper to her, gently rubbing one hand along her back. "I well and truly am."

I feel her nod, then press her face into my neck. A warm, damp feeling tells me she is fighting tears and losing the battle. "It's going to take me a while to sink in," she says. "I shouldn't be so surprised, but still … it was my shop. My clinic. My home. It really is all gone, isn't it?"

"Well … not all of it," Captain Vine breaks in behind us. Amarante and I disengage and turn to see her climbing down from her spot behind the wheel. She unslings the hefty sack from her shoulder as she walks over to us and holds it out to the stricken healer. "We grabbed what we could before we bolted. It's not much, but hopefully it makes up for, um, everything else."

Amarante wipes her eyes on her sleeves and forces a smile as she takes the sack from my Captain. I remove my own from my shoulder and set it down at her feet with an apologetic smile of my own. "I appreciate it, truly," she says to us both, kneeling on the deck in front of both bags. "And … Captain, I apologize for my outburst a moment ago. I didn't know. You're not to blame for my misfortunes."

Captain Vine doesn't answer her, only casts me a quick, unreadable glance before turning her focus back to the bags on the deck.

Momentarily buoyed, Amarante opens the larger sack that my Captain had handed her and digs through it with a hopeful expression on her face. "It may be strange, but this does make me feel somewhat better," she says. "So long as I am not completely without my craft implements, I can … um …"

She trails off, her hand in the sack going still and her face going blank, then blinks a few times down into the open bag.

"What is it?" I ask, worried once more. Did we overlook something vital?

"You …" The healer closes her eyes and sighs, sounding at once exasperated and amused. "You brought *this* of all things, Captain Vine?" she finishes, and pulls her hand from the canvas sack. In it is the long, resin-coated crystal rod with the leather straps that my Captain had asked about the night before.

For reasons I do not understand, I feel a blush begin to form on my cheeks.

"What?" my Captain demands, crossing her arms defiantly beneath her breasts. "You said it was one of the most valuable things you owned, right? So I thought … y'know …"

"Yes, I believe I know exactly what you thought," Amarante replies, standing. She holds the contraption between Captain Vine and herself, both of them looking at it. "And yet … you are right. It is a valuable possession. Smart thinking."

"Thank you," my Captain replies. "So, can we —"

"No," the healer cuts her off, bending and slipping the thing back into the bag. She hefts the both of them, Captain Vine's large one and my smaller one, and turns an imperious gaze on my Captain, who is frowning in disappointment. "At least, not tonight," she adds then, her lips quirking in a small smile. "Perhaps later, I will show you how it is utilized."

My Captain blinks rapidly for a moment, then quirks an eyebrow. "You'll *show* us?" she asks.

Amarante turns around and lets her smile grow larger as she glances at me. "It is the least I can do for the kindness you two have just shown in protecting me and what you could of my valuables," she says, still smiling at me. "And whatever you may think you know of it, Captain Vine, something tells me that Lorelei has mostly no idea what it can do, yes?"

"Mostly," I agree, blushing harder.

"I thought so." Nodding to both of us, the healer crosses the deck to the cabin door. "Then if there are no objections, I'd like to get as settled as I can in the ship's hold near your strange tree. I need to … process all of this, I think. Whenever you think us safely away, Captain Vine, I would appreciate the use of your heartwood talisman again to continue treating my patient. And perhaps, at some time in the near future, I will give you both a lesson on my healing arts."

My Captain and I watch her disappear behind the door, then turn to one another. "I can't believe I just accidentally kidnapped somebody else so soon after you," she says to me.

"You did not kidnap me on accident, Captain," I protest.

She sighs. "Yeah, that's true," she says, and drapes an arm over my shoulder. "Not on accident."

"So what *is* that thing, Captain?" I ask after a moment.

She smirks, her fingers playing with the ends of my hair. "I would tell you, Lei," she says, "but I'd much, much rather just show you. You'll see. Hopefully soon."

"Ah," I say, leaning into her. For a moment, we simply stand with each other on the deck and look up at the clouds passing slowly by in the morning sky. "Captain?" I ask after a moment.

"Hm?" she responds. "Yeah, Lei?"

"It's a not a healing thing, is it?"

"Oh no," she says, then cups my breast in her dangling hand. "Definitely not a healing thing, not for what I got in mind."

I do not even attempt to stop the warmth that spreads in my face. Instead I put my arm around my Captain's hip and rest my hand atop her firm, taut bottom. "Good."

About the Author

D.B. Francais loves complex characters, easy banter, and kinky situations, and can be contacted at dbfrancais@gmail.com for those who wish to send fan mail or suggestions for later episodes, discuss possible writing commissions, or just say hi.

This is the author's second erotic book, and there are plenty more to come. Look for the next episode in *The Queen's Runner* series, *Best Kept Secrets*, available at most online retailers. Please feel free to leave an honest review on Goodreads, Smashwords, or Amazon. You can also follow D.B. Francais on Facebook @queensrunner and on Twitter @dbfrancais. And thanks for reading.

Made in the USA
Columbia, SC
23 February 2023